ALPHA

Nicholas Bruno

ISBN-10: 1508539545
ISBN-13: 978-1508539544

TO MY MOTHER, JOYCE

Contents

ACKNOWLEDGMENTS

My hero.
My Mother

For his support and guidance.
My Father

These three...
Matthew
Christopher
Michael

The Original Darius.
Travis

For making sense of this mess.
Elise Schneider

For the awesome Cover!
Stacey Abraham

A man of education, intellect and enthusiasm.
Sheldon Silver

For the awesome picture!
Scott Grosso

Everyone has that one teacher, who saves a passion and opens a door.
Karli Troisi

In the Beginning...there was space and endless time.

Here and there did not exist, and the difference between darkness and light was absent—everything was connected as one.

Equally and rhythmically this space basked in the still silence, giving off nothing and taking in the same. No thought escaped, no emptiness emerged from its transparent encasing. And so it remained this way.

Then, in a flash—an unknown occurrence. Two nothings collided and created a disturbance. The Being was created. There was nothing to it, no gender, no name, just a wandering spirit. It traveled, marking each moment, taking space and time as Its components. Some thought began to bubble, as the Being began to piece together a long-anticipated puzzle. And so it remained this way.

Each piece collided, creating a spark and igniting such things as faraway stars. As It created, there was still something missing, surely the space that was nothing was filling, but the main feature had yet to surface. Thus the Being called upon something to bring forth a whole new realm. Something so new, so bold and vast, that nothing secondary would thrive or last. For it was perfect and one of a kind. A world of green and blue and curious creature design. The Being let God, his most trusted hand, call forth this world and become protectorate of its lands. Its dwellers would look to Him and He the same, to live together, forever, shielded from pain. And so it was on these seven days, creation created a natural nature nation. And so it remained this way.

God looked to the birds and to the bees, from the trees and their leaves, to the lions and to the lambs. He saw many things and loved them so, but still God thought and thought, and then it was so, a human of flesh, eyes and soul, to make His circle whole. A man by Adam and a woman by Eve took the reins, seeing to it that lives lived would be done so with humility and ease. But it did not remain this way.

The temptation of sin won in the end. A God who was crushed lowered his chin. His image had failed, they would be dismissed. His opposite evil, struck and did not miss. But there was something to be salvaged from this, a way to fix that fatal twist. God turned away from what was now dead, He turned to time, He turned ahead. And so it remained this way, that maybe two souls as one can be and show a battered people what it means to be free.

— Chapter One —

Baker's Bread

It was cold, and in the winter months life seemed without a prayer. I hugged myself as I walked past the closing shops in the town center. The candles in the shops flickered as they were doused one by one by drowsy shop owners preparing to retire for the night. It was quiet and quaint in Ramsford, one of those picture-perfect towns you see in stories.

I looked into one of the windows and saw loaves of bread popping out of baskets and cakes under large and small glass domes. The shop was dark and I was tempted just for a moment to see if the door was unlocked, but the possibility of that was more than unlikely so I brushed the thought to the side. Yanking my head away from the glass to look up to the night sky, where the twinkling of the stars made me feel both small and distant from the big picture. My breath came out in a light fog and my stomach growled. "Maybe tomorrow," I assured my stomach and myself. I turned and the snow beneath me crunched as I continued down the narrow street that cut through the small town.

The sound of a shop bell rang behind me and a person cleared their throat. "I saw you looking through the window, did you want anything?" the voice said. I turned and saw an elderly man, short and with modest clothing—a tan shirt, brown pants, brown boots, and a long white apron covered in flour and icing. His forehead and rosy cheeks were splotched with the white flour that matched winter's snow. It was clear that he often tasted his creations. Bald on top, he did have grandfatherly white muttonchops leading to a full white beard.

"Oh, no thank you." I said simply. I had no money and was not the type to ask for handouts. "Have a nice night, sir." I began to walk down the road again. My nose felt frozen as it started to snow once more. I needed to find somewhere to escape the cold, at least for the night.

I heard the door close behind me. "It was for the best," I kept reassuring myself. "You have nothing to drink anyway so the bread would just make you thirsty." It wasn't uncommon to find myself, from time to time, talking to myself. It probably didn't look sane to onlookers and I realized that, but it sort of helped given the fact that I was alone most of the time nowadays. Two months of travel doesn't seem like much, but without a clear destination, it felt like an eternity. I did have a set goal in mind, however, I did want to find a job and start a new life. From there maybe, just maybe, I could slowly reclaim a somewhat normal existence.

I couldn't have made it more than a few yards before I heard the bustling and crunching of snow behind me. "Excuse me, lad." It was the elderly man again. Why would he want to be out here on this cold and windy night with me, when he can be falling asleep next to the fireplace in the bakery?

"Hello, yes?" I said, trying to keep my teeth from chattering.

"A bit nippy out, isn't it?" He said pulling his coat together while trying to balance a bundle of something between his stomach and his left arm.

"Just a little bit. But, I should be home soon." I flat-out lied. I don't know why I lied to him, it wasn't like he offered me a room above the bakery for the night to get out of cold. I guess I did it, in case he offered me a room above the bakery. I hate to be indebted to people, especially since I have nothing to give back.

He looked at me and smirked. "Home for you is a long way away. Here, take this." The man handed me the bundle, warm and tightly folded. It was just as I feared and even though my stomach and mind screamed **"food"** my heart had too much pride to accept such a gift. "How do you know that? And sorry, I can't accept this." I tried to give the bundle back but the man stopped me.

"I see in your eyes that you are lost, and don't give me the runaround about not accepting a gift. I know you are trying to prove yourself as a young man in a harsh world. But believe me lad, it only gets worse when you're an old geezer like me, so accept the help when help comes calling. Listen, take this too." The old man handed me a full canteen.

"Thanks, but no thanks." I tried once more to give it back to the old man but he did not budge. "Listen, I appreciate the gesture but I am fine." I said growing frustrated. He laughed.

"You are fine? You didn't see the expression on your face when you looked into my shop window." He rested his hand on my shoulder. "Going through life alone, whether for a few days or for an entirety makes no difference. The difference only arises when a friend comes along the way to lend a hand." The old man stepped back and the snow started to pick up.

"Wait! What's your name?" I shouted as a gust of wind hit me.

"Its Edmund," he called out before disappearing into the developing storm.

"Thank you" I called back, the bundle starting to cool in my hands. I took my pack off and stuffed it inside. It was important I find somewhere warm to spend the night, then I'd eat. I'll admit I was very fortunate to have the run-in with Edmund; he was kind and his gift would keep me in good health and in good spirits for a long time. But I still wasn't thrilled about having to accept such a kind gesture because now I felt like I couldn't make it on my own in this world.

It might have been a few hours but I knew it was only a few minutes and already I was ready to collapse. The snow was falling faster and faster and getting harder and harder to walk through. I was getting colder as each second ticked by. I succumbed and my knees hit the ground. It was too cold to keep moving. Crystals seared my face as I winced into the icy wind.

"Help," I involuntarily whimpered, just before everything went dark.

I was falling, but I wasn't moving. I could hear and feel a rushing sound all around me. I couldn't see anything except for a fuzzy image that swirled around my line of sight, more or less making me feel as though I was drowning. Was this what dying felt like? I knew my body was laying in the snow somewhere, just around the corner from Edmund's shop. Oh, how I wish he would find me here.

With the same sudden feeling of falling, I suddenly felt myself being raised up and carried. Was I ascending into heaven? No, I couldn't be dead, could I? A deep depression set in, as if a mile high wave was crashing down on me. All my life I have done nothing but wander. When I was stationary, I wandered in my thoughts, always with the feeling of being unfulfilled. How I wished to start this journey all over at that moment, to find some purpose along the way.

I was feeling warmth now. I wasn't ascending or descending anymore, simply lying down. I felt my mind rock back and forth into a calm, quiet, peaceful place. A place where my dreams greet me at the gates.

"Can you hear the curious sound, when mysterious chatter, and people for that matter, are around? Can't help but wonder, is that the crackle of thunder? Or the warning sound. Have no fear, we are here, all dots to be connected. All waiting to defend what is to be resurrected." An echo of a man's voice bounced up and down a long dark room. The room was moving —in fact, it swayed from side to side just enough for one to notice and every once in a while it gave a small hop. My eyes opened slightly and were met by a glowing light. Where in the world was I? I was warm, covered by blankets. However, I still couldn't make out the room I was in and now with someone strange close by, I grew uneasy.

"Don't be afraid, I saved you don't-cha know, about dead you were." The same voice said very matter of fact. One small lantern perched on a crate was all that separated us. I looked past the glowing light and saw the silhouette of a man. He turned the lantern up, then came into full focus. He wore many layers of ripped and patched clothing, including a fuzzy hat with flaps, and tiny traces of golden hair stuck out in all directions. His face was smudged with black streaks. His eyes were bight blue and he had a comforting smile. He held in his hand a can of beans with a spoon sticking out. His boots were worn and his pants torn and sewed in patches. He was one of a kind in my book. I looked around and suddenly I knew where I was—a box car.

"Who are you?" I groaned sitting up. I suddenly felt all the aches and soreness in my body.

"The name is Neo, and you?"

"Barnaby. How did I get here?" I groaned again.

"I brought you here." Neo said cheerfully.

"Why?" I asked.

"Well, you were lying on the ground and I didn't have the heart to leave you there." Neo said, laughing at me. "So, I picked you up and decided to take you with me until I knew you were okay to continue on your own."

"Thanks. Listen I have some bread and water if you want it, you're more then welcome." It was the least I could do, I mean the guy didn't even know me and he did so much to help me.

"Nah, I'm good. I got enough, you should eat though. You look like you're about to faint." I hesitated for a moment. "Well, go ahead." Neo laughed.

I ripped into the bag and then the bundle of bread, taking the biggest bite out of one of the three loves Edmund had given me. Then I look two giant gulps of water before I slowed down to catch my breath. I let out a sigh of relief and put my head back, resting it on the box car's cold steel wall.

"Tell me about yourself," I asked Neo. He had such an interesting presence about him, like he had so many stories and secrets.

"Well, I am a fairly simple man. I am just like you. Looking for a place where I can wait out the storm," he said softly.

"What?" It didn't seem like Neo was talking about the weather. He cleared his throat.

"Well, to be frank everything has gone to shit around here, in case you haven't noticed. I'm not one to believe in conspiracies, but I do have a feeling something big is about to happen, ya' know? Something that is going to test the people's faith."

"You think the people's faith will be strong enough to test?" I joked.

Neo put his spoon into the can and rested it on the floor

14

beside him. He sat up and folded his knees, draping his arms over them so he could lean forward.

"Well, that all depends on which side they take. We have a saying where I come from, it goes something like this. 'Faith is nothing more than the capability to see past doubt.' "

"You seem to have things figured out. Just out of curiosity, do you have anything to say about those who have been blinded by false faith?" I tried to see his point but something in my past prevented me from doing so.

Neo smiled. "Yes, in fact we do. Faith does not thrive off the mortal aspect of sight, for faith is the feeling of what isn't there but what is the only thing present." Then Neo leaned back, picked up his can, and continued eating.

"You sound funny, you know that? Its like you speak in a rhythm," I joked.

"It's a hobby." Neo smirked.

"I take it you have a strong faith then?" I continued, surprised that someone with so little was defending such a thing. I mean he was sitting in rags in a boxcar, eating out of an old can of beans.

"Faith is different from my perspective as it is for everyone. Sometimes people treat the world as if it were God's house, others only have faith on game day. It is each individual's right to chose where their loyalties lie when it comes to their relationship with Him." He pointed upward as he continued eating.

"What are you, a philosopher?" I asked. Neo grinned.

"No, no, no. But thank you for the compliment, or was it a clever dig?" he asked.

"It was a compliment." It was a nice break from the 'why me' attitude that I usually encountered. "So what else is there about you, Neo?" I was trying to change the subject. Not that I didn't want to talk about the topic of faith, but I was one of those whom Neo talked about. I'd only gone to church a handful of times in my life and when I did, I didn't feel as though I was connected to God in any special way.

"I'm an open book, ask away." He was very friendly.

"Well all right, why are you here? Where are you going?" Usually, when people ride in box cars they are trying to start anew, they try and find opportunity along the tracks.

"May I give you some advice, Barnaby?" Neo asked.

"Uh, sure." I wasn't really expecting someone in Neo's position to be giving advice, although under the circumstances I'd say I needed it. Plus who was I to judge?

"Never stay idle. It gives you a chance to weigh the odds." Neo's point was very true. When trapped, I'm often found in a heated argument with myself over the smallest things.

"That is a good way to look at life." I said knowing I could benefit tremendously from heeding Neo's words. "You didn't answer my question, though."

"You caught me," he laughed. "I am simply going along for the ride, hiding in the steerage until I am called home." Neo answered things in a funny way.

"Do you have family waiting for you there? I asked.

"Yes, I have an extensive family waiting for me…" Neo trailed off with a stare that went on for thousands of miles. A moment dragged by before I began to worry.

"Neo? We don't have to talk about it if you don't want to," I said gently.

"Who, what?" Neo looked back at me. "Oh, sorry, Barnaby. To answer your question: I do have a family, a large one, in fact; they're all waiting."

Knowing that was about all Neo was going to give me I didn't press the conversation too much farther, but that didn't stop him from asking me the same question.

"How about you? Any family?" He took another spoonful of beans.

Neo and I had something in common; it was hard for us to talk about our families. However, I slowly answered nonetheless. "No, well yes. I assume everyone has a family." I took another swig of water. "My father was always away, he was loving though and my mother stayed home. She was one to always smile, she was beautiful…"

I stopped and found myself in the same thousand-mile stare that Neo had used before. I was unlocking the box of my past that I had bolted shut on purpose. The horror I was beginning to see suddenly amplified and took control over me. I heard Neo say my name but it was only in a muffled tone. I looked around the car and then back down towards the lantern light. Neo said my name once more, but still it was just white noise.

I continued whether I wanted to or not—my body needed me to. "We always went to church on Sunday, my mother, and my older brother Marshall. My father would join us once a month when he had the weekend off. One day we were all in church and during the sermon, Marshall excused himself to go to the bathroom. A couple minutes later there was a loud sound from outside. One of the members of the congregation went outside to see where the noise came from and all the while I had a weird feeling in my stomach. It wasn't until we heard a scream from outside that my suspicions were confirmed. Marshall had -". I stopped myself, staring blankly into my lap. A knot formed in my throat but I refused to cry, I convinced myself I couldn't long ago.

"He...?" Neo asked.

"He jumped." I finished

The silence inside the car was deafening. My breathing was shallow as it held back whatever foreign emotion was bubbling up inside me.

"Do you believe he jumped on purpose?" Neo asked.

I looked up, that was the first time anyone has ever asked me that question. I have asked that myself though many, many times and each time I had a hunch that he didn't. But still my mind searched for anything that held reason.

The feeling that I locked away that day, as everyone ran

into the courtyard of the church while I just sat there on the pew, tapped itself on my shoulder and whispered into my ear causing pain to trickle down my spine.

"No, why would he?" I managed to get out. Then the emotion that was bubbling up inside me erupted. It wasn't tears or sadness, it just was confusion in its purest form. "He was smart and funny. He was handsome and all the girls in school loved him. He was determined and his goals were set. His friends looked up to him and he was friends with everyone and anyone, not for social status but for the pure enjoyment of another's company. He was gentle and soft-spoken but commanded any room he walked into like he was a general. He was happy too, genuinely happy. I swear to it, because he showed it. He was all the good I hoped to be, he was....he was my brother and I didn't even get to say good bye." I paused and let out a short ironic laugh, "The last thing I said to him was **lucky,** because he was leaving right before the priest who was known for the really long homilies." I noticed I had started to shake.

"I'm sorry, Barnaby—I can't possibly imagine what that did to you."

"Your relationship with God seems strong—mine has vanished. I sat in that pew for hours, no one could move me. Everything was in slow motion. I sat there in silence asking for the day to rewind itself, but nothing." I slowed down my pace and took a deep breathe. "The burial was later that week and even the priest didn't know what to say. My father turned into a drunk

19

almost immediately afterwards and my mother never smiled again. Their deaths were months later, they died from broken hearts. I guess you can say it was a blessing for my mother's sake. No one should lose a child."

"It is a shame though, they were so blinded by grief that they couldn't see that I was still there." It was like everything was falling out at once. "You know I tried to off myself even, but I couldn't even do that, so I took the easy way out and left everything behind. Knowing the pain would drown me like it did my parents. It looks like it has followed me here. You know, I'm starting to think that you should have left me out there in the snow."

Neo sat silently. If I were him, I wouldn't know what to say either. I had put him in an awkward position, no doubt. Here I was spilling my guts to a total stranger because he bore a slight resemblance to my dead brother.

"I can't promise the past. I can't ensure the present, but I can tell you the future holds so much more for you so please, just hold on. If not for you, then for Marshall." Neo said with assurance.

"I tell myself something similar. 'Always remember and never surrender.' In a way it gives me strength. Neo, I have a confession that I never told anyone else before." Then my emotion reached its apex. "I don't think what happened on that day was real. A part of me is still searching for the truth. Like I know it happened and that he is dead but, but, I don't know—it's hard to explain."

"You'll find that truth one day, Barnaby. I believe in you." Neo smiled and then reached into his overcoat pocket. He handed me a small grey object. It was stone and slightly bigger than my palm. "What is it?" I asked looking from it to Neo.

"Its name is Elek, it is a gargoyle. Think of it as a companion. It wards off evil."

"Elek, I like that name." I said, cheering up. The small gargoyle had its wings wrapped around itself. Its face looked like a mix between a ram and a lion. As I held Elek in my hand, I felt strength and safety. It felt right.

"Good, I'm glad you like him." Neo said smiling. "He's all yours."

"I can't accept this—" I began, but Neo wasn't having a useless debate with me.

"No it's yours," he insisted.

"So, where are we going?" I asked.

"Well, the next stop is a small town called Gideon. You'll be getting off there."

"But, I want to stay here and travel with you." I said sounding a tad childish.

"Sorry Barnaby, that isn't in the cards for now, I know Gideon, you'll find refuge there. They are good people and they are very welcoming. Someday our paths will cross again. As for now, let's get some rest; we're arriving there tomorrow and you don't want to miss this stop."

Neo went over to the lantern and turned it down. I packed the remaining loaves of bread the canteen of water back into my pack and laid down. My eyes became heavy and I slipped away into the night.

"We have to act now." A young, frustrated man's voice stated.

"In time." A calm and gentle voice exclaimed, this voice sounded much older.

"We have to meet this, fire with fire. Don't You realize that?" The young voice demanded.

"I know." The older voice was still calm. "He will be that fire."

"You know, I have never trusted children with fire." The voice sounded disappointed with the other voice's answer. The candle flickered and then extinguished itself.

The train whistle blew. We were arriving at the Gideon station.

— Chapter Two —
A Girl Worth Fighting For

The boxcar as well as the rest of the train came to a screeching halt right outside the Gideon station. Even though no passengers were getting on or off, supplies were flowing to and from the train with the same commotion. This gave Neo and I the opportunity to sneak off the box car with two small crates and onto the platform. After setting them down into a wagon that was to be carted off to the market, Neo turned to me and extended his hand.

"Well, my dear friend, it seems we have come to a crossroads. I can honestly say that you will be just fine. My only advice to you now is to make friends, you never know when they might just save your life." We both laughed.

"Yeah I'll try." I said back. I still felt silly about being so open with Neo, but he seemed cool about it.

The train whistle blew and everyone on the platform scrambled to get the last of the crates off the train. Neo slipped back into the boxcar. "Always remember to keep Elek with you! He comes in handy when you least expect it."

"I will! Thank you," I shouted back not really knowing what he meant. All the same I really hoped that we would meet again.

I walked to the edge of the platform that faced a twisting

muddy road. The last of the wagons was preparing to leave for town. "Hey, do you think I could get a ride?" I called to the driver.

"Sure, but hurry down," the man muttered.

I jumped off the platform and made a beeline for the wagon. I sat in the back with the crates to make sure they didn't fall off. I was off to Gideon.

I couldn't believe the luck I've had in just the past twenty four hours. If Neo was even half right about this being a good place for me, than maybe my dream of finally having a home again would become reality.

The sun beamed down on me as I finished the rest of the food Edmund had given me. I slipped the now-empty canteen back into my bag. The road was bumpy and since it was particularly warmer than yesterday, the snow from the previous night was starting to melt. This made the wagon's journey to Gideon slow down.

"Hey kid." The diver turned around from where he was sitting.

"Yes?" I said turning to him as well.

"Get out and push the cart, we're stuck," his voice was monotone.

"Sure." I said back as I took my pack off and placed it on top of the nearest crate. What happened next I pretty much asked for. While the wagon was moving I had my feet dangling off the end, so when I went to get off I just jumped off carelessly instead of turning around to climb down. I underestimated the amount of mud on the path and the second I hit the ground my feet slipped out from underneath me and I landed right on my back. I instantly felt a dull pain all over and felt a thick, wet layer of mud on my backside.

"Quit fooling around." Called the driver.

Groaning, I pulled myself up and started to push. Unfortunately I had no traction and was more slipping than pushing. It took ten minutes and a few irritated comments from the driver until we were on our way again. I was more or less miserable after that, but knowing that we were almost there made it better.

It was well into the afternoon when we arrived into town. The other wagons were almost done unloading their crates. Some of the other men came over after they were finished to help the driver and I unpack the wagon. I thought that was very nice of them. I was tired and dirty from the day and now I needed to figure out what my next steps were going to be. It was clear I needed a place to stay, I quickly remembered Neo's advice before he left—I should make a friend if I am to start my new life here.

"Hey, thanks a lot, kid. Sorry, about before, I had a deadline and I needed to make it to get paid in full. I'm Jason by the way". He said extending his hand.

"Its okay, don't worry about it. I'm Barnaby." I shook Jason's hand.

Jason was dark skinned. He wore a vest and a white shirt that was rolled up at the sleeves, his shirt was tucked into tan pants, and his boots were splotched with fresh mud. His eyes were light brown and his hair was dark and short. A beard covered his full face.

"Here is something for your troubles." Jason handed me a small pouch. It made a clinking sound.

"You gave me a ride here; that's payment enough." I refused and handed him back the gift.

"No, take it. I ruined your clothes so consider this payment for getting us out of the mud. Besides if I hired a highway hand, I would have to completely split my pay with him and I couldn't afford that ." I went to interject but he stopped me again. "At least go to the inn and get cleaned up."

"All right, thank you again." I finally gave into receiving the money.

"See you around, Barnaby." Jason climbed back onto the cart and headed off back down the road with the other merchants.

The marketplace was swarming with shop keepers who began to unpack their respective deliveries. Here was no place for me; the money I was given was going to put to good use at the inn. The town was similar to Ramsford. The architecture matched almost identically, there were small wooden homes and shops, and the cobblestone street felt the same below my feet. I liked it, I have always been a fan of the simplicity and the humble atmosphere of the life outside the big cities that have sprouted up around the country. To me, they feel like two different worlds.

Truth be told, they ARE two different worlds. Through

recent political action and climate change, the shifting of the population has split the country entirely. What was once the United States of America is now a three-region skeleton of what it used to be. The Confederate Conference of America, as it is now known, can only dream about filling the shoes of the United Nation that once stood in the age before the war. We are divided as a people and that doesn't help our hopes of returning to our former glory.

In the cities, people bask in wealth and ultimate luxury. Out in the northeastern settlements is the moderation of hard-working families. They live off of what they grow and buy from local marketplaces. I was raised in one of these towns, and have only heard stories of the cities that lie on the shore lines to the south.

The climate has changed due to factors created by man but are now beyond his control. The midwest has become harsh and prone to extremes. In the northeast, the people enjoy lush springs and summers, bountiful harvests, and winters where the plentiful population of various animals provides pelts and food.

The people around here refer to the cities in the south as "sinful cities" but officially these states are called the "united conference states." The nickname is not tied to religion as much as one thinks, but there is a certain truth to it all. The northeast is referred to the "eastern bounty states" and the midwest is known as the "baron states." It is said that there are tribes in these states, people who managed to live in the constantly changing, unforgiving climate, but they keep to themselves and have remained off the radar for half a century. They are the stuff of folk lore in our country.

However, climate change alone is not the only reason that these events occurred. Back before I was born and many others in fact, there was a world war that came to be known as the Purging Wars. It lasted for many years and destroyed vast amounts of land, making many miles simply uninhabitable. The governments of the world evacuated people from these dangerous areas, known as "blackout zones"—places where even when the sun was shinning the ruins of bombings left the land in constant silence and darkness. It was as if sound itself was sucked into a black hole .

In the south, however, there was peace. Opportunity for businesses of all kinds started to pick up because with war comes demand, and entrepreneurship thrives on that concept. Surprisingly, the worst area during this war was in what are now known as the eastern bounty states. These states were scorched, the wildfires lasted for months, and all life was driven from the land. The northern most part of the country was in tatters and the south didn't do anything but watch as the bombs dropped, and the manmade climate-yielding weapons made life unruly.

Then something happened. The war ended just like that. It seemed to good to be true but no one can say what factor led to peace. Everyone agrees that it ended because there was simply no one left to fight. With more than seventy-five percent of the world's population destroyed, many feared that man kind wouldn't have a bright future, or even a future at all.

On the one-year anniversary of peace, it started to rain in the eastern states for the first time. Despite the odds, nature returned, stronger than ever. Few returned, fearing of another war; many stayed in their comfortable lives in the south. But, the ones who went back to their roots were determined to respect the land that they still loved. In fact the very first settlement built after the resettlement was dubbed Phoenix, after the mythical bird who resurrects after a fiery death, and so the heart of the east began to beat once more.

I walked down the inn's creaky stairs. The inn was on the second floor of a pub called "Day's Pay," named apparently after the original owner noticed that the workers would go directly from the lumber yards and mines to the pub after the sun had set.

I decided to use the two coins I had left to get something to eat. Jason had given me more than I thought—not only enough for a bath and for my clothes to be properly washed, but enough so that I could stay the night and have dinner. I wish he hadn't given me so much but I was quite comfortable and the guilt trailed off as I smelled the warm, hearty soup from the cauldron over the large fireplace. Edmund's advice came dancing back into my thoughts, **"believe me lad, it only gets worse, so accept the help when help comes calling."** Maybe he was right; maybe I shouldn't be so hesitant about letting people in, letting people help me when I clearly need it.

The pub was a decent-sized room with many tables that

had no particular layout. Each table had two chairs on opposite ends and a lit candle in the middle, making for dim but sufficient lighting. Patrons either drank at the bar or huddled around each other laughing and telling stories. It was nice, and cozy. The fire not only enhanced the smell of the soup but it also left the room warm, with the effect of hypnotism as it comforted you into a dreamlike state.

"What will you have?" asked a woman's voice as I took a seat at one of the many tables.

I looked up and froze, as she was the most beautiful girl I had ever seen. Her brown eyes caught both imagination and wonderment like two unknown galaxies meeting you after eternal travel through space's deep and vast emptiness. Her features were smooth and gentle. She was elegant—she reminded me of the princess in a story my mom used to tell me. Her brown hair flowed into a loose braid that trailed down just past her shoulder and onto her chest. Her voice was sweet and calm but with a certain independence and confidence that leads me to believe that she handles herself quite well in any situation. She wore a simple housedress, which was very different from the complex, overdone dresses they wear in the city. This was form fitting, more conservative but still flattering. As I looked at her I suddenly realized that somehow everything I was searching for in my journey was fulfilled in her gaze.

"What will you have?" she said again, looking at me like I was insane.

Trying to keep my face from flushing, I composed myself. "I'll have whatever that smell is," I spat out in a quirky manner, "and some tea."

She looked at me and smiled. "All right, I'll be right back."

A few minutes passed and then she returned with my order—a steaming bowl of soup with a piece of bread and a small chipped tea cup with a small pot of tea. I handed her the two coins and she slipped them into the center pocket of her apron that she wore over her dress. "Enjoy," she said as she turned to leave.

"Would you like to join me?" I asked. "You don't have to, but I am new to this town and well, I could use a friend."

She looked at me with suspicion. "That's very sweet of you, but I'm working. Plus you travelers are all alike, I know the whole 'new in town' routine." She turned away again. My mind raced for another approach.

I stood up and walked around to the other side of the table, I pulled out the wooden chair, "Please, I am not going to try anything. I just thought you could use someone to talk to who hasn't been drinking all night."

She turned around once more and smiled. She brought her hand to her face and moved a piece of hair to the side which had fallen in front of it. "Fine, but if you try anything—"

"I won't, I give you my word." I was quick to say this, she looked at me for a moment as if she was processing me, making sure I past some mental test she concocted.

"Okay. Just give me a minute." She walked over to the bar and fixed herself another bowl of soup and brought over another cup of tea. She sat down and I pushed her in. "Well, you're a gentleman." She joked ripping off some bread and dunking it into the soup.

"I try, I haven't really had the opportunity to do this with someone for a very long time." I said, taking a seat.

"This is by no means a date." she quickly stated.

"No, of course not. I just miss having someone around." Her company was enough for me.

"Oh. Well, glad I can be that company. I'm Annabelle by the way, Annabelle West." She lifted up her teacup.

"And I'm Barnaby, Barnaby Maverick." I picked up mine as well and there was a small clink as we tapped our cups together.

"That's quite a name." She smiled and I blushed.

"Yeah, I am not sure why I was named Barnaby, it's kind of dumb."

She began to laugh, "Yes, it is."

"Oh." I muttered.

"It's a good type of silly." She rested her hand on mine. I started blushing so I looked away. "What's the matter?" she asked sweetly.

"Nothing, nothing at all." I tried to change the subject but my mind went blank—she was so beautiful.

"You're weird," she smirked, then she began to eat. Throughout the meal we exchanged jokes and some stories about our past. I didn't tell her anything I'd told Neo, though; I didn't want those feelings coming up again, especially since I was finally feeling that I was moving on and that I had a chance here.

"Another round, sweetheart." A man yelled from the bar. Annabelle didn't move, however, she just sipped her tea.

"Anyway, so aside from traveling alone and those people helping you along the way, what else is there? What about your family?" She continued with our conversation, completely ignoring the drunken request from across the bar.

How was I going to tell her my past without actually bringing up my past? I ran away from it basically, trying to leave the demons that haunted my dreams behind instead of confronting them. "Well…" my thoughts trailed off and I found myself looking into the now-empty bowl.

"I said another round, sweetheart " I heard footsteps behind me. "Is this your boyfriend?" I turned around and a burly man was right there, towering over me. His arms were as big as his belly, he was also bald and reeked of whiskey. He was a mean-looking man and either worked as a lumberjack or a blacksmith— both options made him equally intimidating. He had a tan shirt that probably was white at some point and wore jeans with suspenders. His muddy boots were loud as they stomped over the old wooden floor.

"I think you've had enough." Annabelle said, sipping on her tea with no enthusiasm.

"Here's what's going to happen love, how's about you fix

us all another round and then why don't we have a proper introduction." His smile was more or less unpleasant and his breath was even worse.

"The only proper introduction you will be getting is with the floor if you don't leave now. You have had enough and unless you want to spend the rest of the night in prison or worse, there's the door." She gestured with her head as she sipped the tea yet again.

Before I could react the man pushed me off the chair, knocking me to the ground. Annabelle reacted in less then a second, taking her tea cup and splashing it into the face of the drunk. He screamed as he tried to wipe his eyes. Now in blind fury, he grabbed the table and flipped it over, but this just made things worse for him. In one graceful move Annabelle ran up and swept him clean off his feet with a kick to the back of his leg. I don't know how she moved so fast, but the bar was now silent and everyone was looking at the scene. Only the crackle of the fire could be heard.

She moved the piece of hair that had fallen in front of her face once more and looked down at the man. "I warned you. Now, get out; you're done for tonight." She then scanned the room. "That goes for the rest of you." Everyone without question took a last swig of their drinks and left. A few of the man's friends helped him up, bringing him towards the door. His head was still spinning as he stumbled out into the crisp, cold night.

"That was impressive." I said, helping her turn the table

right side up.

"That happens about once or twice a month, I don't hold it against them. Most of the people who come here either work in the forests or mines." She untied her apron and set it down on the table.

After an awkward pause I realized I was looking into her eyes, she looked back at me in response with an uncomfortable glance. "All right well, goodnight." I turned around and made my way to the back of the pub where the stairs were that lead to the rooms on the second floor of the inn.

Shutting the door to the small room I stumbled to the bed, collapsing in the clean sheets. I hadn't slept in an actual bed since I left my home. Admittedly, I can see now that I planned my journey poorly, and nearly killed myself a half dozen times in the process.

But, that was all behind me now. I was safe here in Gideon. Well, as safe as I could be, considering I wasn't here a full day and I'd already been caught in a brawl with a drunken stranger. But I wasn't alone, was I? Annabelle was there to restore the peace, even though she enforced it with violence. She handled herself with total grace and elegance but remained firm and swift. It was a combination that I wasn't accustomed to—it mesmerized me. I was saved by a girl and I wasn't ashamed in the least. With thoughts of her and my next move, I slipped into a well-needed sleep.

Tap. Tap. Tap. Footsteps on granite rose above a

bustling noise of different sounds. Then another pair, another person perhaps? Two feet appeared in the mist of the darkness, then to the pair's right appeared another pair, this pair however wore heels instead of black dress shoes. Was this a couple? Where were they going? Who were they? More tapping slowly started to rise in volume as three more sets of footsteps emerged from the darkness. Two of them wore the same black shoes as the first and another wore boots with a slight heel. Suddenly, a floor came into focus.

The sets of feet were all moving in unison and in a V formation. Then they stopped. The lead had set its foot into what looked like an embedded footprint; it was the perfect fit. The other noises that filled the air all hushed now. All the feet disappeared and the lower half of a man's face appeared. He smiled and it curled my stomach, but why? "Well, if the shoe fits." He began to laugh and so did the others. A baby started to cry as the laugher and the screams fought to be loudest. The face vanished and a teddy bear with spots of blood dotting it fell for miles, finally hitting the ground and shattering into millions of pieces.

— Chapter Three —

Eastern Bounty State

Jolting awake in a cold sweat was not how I wanted to wake up. The image of the bizarre and unexplainable dream still burned into my eyes. Every time I blinked I swore I could see the teddy bear and the man's smile. What the hell could it mean? Even with little faith, I was still a firm believer in everything having meaning and a purpose. Even if lately the meanings of things led to pain and misfortune. Even if that reason couldn't be explained just at that moment; nothing was two dimensional, nothing was black and white.

Shaking off what I could from the fresh haze of confusion, I got myself together and prepared for the day ahead. There were multiple things I had to do and I didn't have time to waste. The first thing I had to do was to find a job and I had to do it quickly. I had spent all the money Jason was gracious enough to give me and if I were to spend another night in the inn I would need some form of income in order to do so.

The smell of the soup and the warm hug from the heat of the fire enveloped me once more as I walked down into the pub below the inn. There were one or two patrons at the tables chatting. Annabelle was huddled in the corner of the bar with a man taller than I. Walking over to them, I thought about what to say to Annabelle in order to thank her for the hospitality. As I approached them I heard a faint voice that belonged to a woman.

"Oh, hi Barnaby." Annabelle said after she turned around to set her mug onto the bar. "Barnaby, this is Darius, Darius Crow. He is a police officer in town." The man turned around; he was stocky and well kept. He had a gentleman's appeal and he carried himself with respect and dignity. His uniform was that of the EBS (Eastern Bounty State) Troopers. He wore several medals that showed his years of service, marksmanship, and acts of valor. His gold hair was flipped up and combed to the side. "Hello Barnaby, how are you?" he said with an underlying confidence and charm.

"Hello, I am fine thanks, yourself?" I responded. For the first time a person's mere presence made me feel small. Every insecurity I had seemed to tap my shoulder as if to remind me that they were there. It wasn't a nice feeling.

Before Darius could answer, the woman's voice began to speak again. The two of them turned to a small dusty television that sat in the corner of the bar. A faded picture of a woman from one of the "Sin City" states sat behind a desk with a small stack of papers. Her hair was in a fancy swirl and she wore a bright red dress that matched her lips.

"This just in," the women began. "Updates on the incident inside Germany's Munich Cathedral. Earlier today, screams were heard within the building. Witnesses in the surrounding area said they tried to open the doors but found that they were locked." She took a pause as she flipped to the next page. "After the screams stopped the doors unlocked and witnesses discovered sixty-six bodies."

The women looked up and cleared her throat, then continued slowly. "An inside source says that one survivor was found clutching a stuffed bear. The man kept muttering 'Der Teufelstritt' before he died minutes later."

"Yikes." Darius let out as Annabelle put her hand to her mouth. The news reporter continued.

"Officials are still investigating the cause of the deaths and who can be behind it. But, already there have been a few theories as religious groups show up to the area shouting that the end is not near but in fact here. This is Heather Moss reporting for Channel Six news."

Darius turned off the TV and turned to both Annabelle and me. "Very disturbing and peculiar."

"Nothing peculiar about it. Probably some religious nut who went crazy. Or some sick person who wanted to watch the controversy, throw everyone into a panic." Annabelle answered back flatly.

"You're probably right." Darius hesitantly answered.

"Anyway, you should get going, I have a lot to do today so unless you're going to help-".

"No, no. I have to get going anyway, I have several stops along my patrol today so I should get to it. Good day, Annabelle."

"Good day, officer. Oh, and take Barnaby with you, I don't want him hanging around here getting in my way."

Darius looked me over, "Sure, we're short-handed. I guess

I can find something for him to do. Okay, lets go." Darius beckoned for me and I followed him outside. The streets of Gideon were bustling as the newly filled markets sold goods to the locals. The social atmosphere was refreshing and crisp. But, that wasn't the only thing that was different about today. It was warm and the birds were chirping a new song, it was like nature was welcoming spring.

Since the peace, the climate had altered; this was because the weapons used in the wars had defied nature. The winter months became less harsh in this region than they used to be. Up until the Purging Wars, snow used to rule from the end of November to the end of February; but with the tampering of weather patterns to inflict damage and suffering onto a specific region, the four seasons have shifted slightly. The winter months still begin at the end of November but now end in January, Spring begins afterward and ends in mid July while Summer is shortened, spanning to mid August, Fall is squeezed into the slot that remains.

"Ah, the beginnings of Spring." Darius took a deep breath in and let it out. "Not a bad winter if I do say so myself."

"Yeah." even though I was enjoying the atmosphere I still had a underlying feeling of inferiority around Darius. I think it was his personality—he had charisma and a sense of nobility that I hoped for.

"All right, so I'll go through the checklist with you for today. Usually I don't bring strangers on patrols, heck I don't bring anyone on patrols, but I can make an exception this one time. You seem harmless." He laughed, and even his laugh had a certain command to it. I looked down and shuffled my feet as I walked. How was I supposed to keep up with someone like this?

"Come now, don't look sloppy. You are a trainee for Gideon's patrol and I'll be damned if one of my recruits is out of order. Speaking of sloppy, you need a uniform and a haircut," he paused, "no offense."

"None taken." I answered running my fingers through my scruffy hair.

"Well, if there are no objections then let's make a few stops before we start our day." Darius turned on the spot and walked down one of the small streets that sprouted out from the marketplace. We walked for no more than a few minutes before we came to a small wooden building. Darius immediately walked up to the door, straightened his uniform and walked inside. I was left outside confused and in a state of being out of place.

Darius appeared in the doorway and chuckled, "well come on in. You still want that haircut, right?"

"Oh, yeah, right." I quickly walked into the building trying to play off any embarrassment.

The room was long, well lit, and had four barber seats all facing mirrors. There were razors and scissors neatly placed on the counter and everything was spotless. On the wall hung some pictures, but what caught my eye almost immediately was the shadow box. Inside the shadow box was a shirt that appeared to be the uniform top of an EBS Trooper. It was highly decorated, even more so than the one Darius wore. Also instead of being green it was a deep blue. It was impressive, to say the least.

"Like it?" A deep voice called from the back of the barber's shop.

"Hello Sir, just the man I wanted to see." Darius smiled and walked over with his hand extended, the two embraced.

"Looking good, I see you were promoted. Sorry I couldn't make it. I was in Hudson burying an old buddy." The man smiled. He was stocky and had greying hair. He also had a mustache and a belly but other than that he looked ordinary.

"I am sorry to hear that, I am sure he was a good man." I responded.

"A better one than I. Recruited him myself you know, saved my life a few times when we had those problems with smugglers from the south."

"Speaking of recruits, I brought one by for a cleanup today. Came into town yesterday looking for a job, is staying over at the inn." Darius gestured to me. "Barnaby, this is Colonel Reynolds, Sir this is Barnaby."

"For the last time call me Ed, I'm enjoying my retirement. Pleased to meet you, son." Ed shook my hand with a tight grip. "All right lad, take a seat."

I looked into the mirror and to my surprise I looked worse than I thought. My hair was askew and my clothes were disheveled.

"So Darius, I take it you want me to give him the usual?"
Ed asked Darius, who was eyeing the uniform that hung on the
wall.

"Yeah, I am going to take him along with me today."
Darius half answered back; he was really enamored with the
uniform.

Ed laughed at a mesmerized Darius, then turned to me.
"So Barnaby, tell me about yourself. What brings you to Gideon?"
Ed began snipping away. Hairs fell like leaves on a windy fall day.

"Well, there is not much to tell. I'm looking for work and a
place to live, basically. On my way here a friend suggested that I
settle in Gideon; said it's safe and there is a lot of opportunity
here."

"Damn right its safe, between Darius and the other
Troopers this place is like a fortress." He smiled at me through the
mirror and patted me firmly on the shoulder.

I sat there for the rest of the haircut in silence, Ed and
Darius went back and forth like old buddies. I chimed in every so
often with a simple one- or two-word answers when I was asked a
question or my opinion. I wasn't focused though; I kept thinking
back to Annabelle. I really wanted to see her again. I wanted the
chance to make another first impression. I know that I didn't look
that desirable when the drunken man pushed me aside like I was
nothing but if I could come off as someone who is strong and
who can take care of himself, then I could stop looking like a
wounded animal in front of her.

"All right, all done." Ed turned the chair around and I looked at myself in the mirror. Clean-cut and now presentable, a smile appeared on my face.

This is going to impress Annabelle, I thought to myself.

"Thank you," I said standing up shaking Ed's hand once again.

"No problem, you're a fine lad and I am glad to see that the force is growing. Take care and good luck." Ed walked us out of the small barber shop and we parted. Darius and I were off down the alley once again, I could feel for the first time in a while the slight breeze on my ears.

"Just one more stop and then we will be off on our patrol." Darius said carrying himself in a fashion that was admirable and fresh. He must have looked up to Ed a lot. I know I was starting to.

"How many Troopers are there?" I asked trying to mimic and keep up with Darius' steps.

"In Gideon there are forty members of the EBS Trooper Corps." Darius proudly answered.

"What rank are you?" I asked curiously looking at the patch that was carefully and neatly sewn onto his jacket.

"We follow the old world military rank system. These stripes mean I am a Sergeant Major, Ed is a Colonel, his insignia was a bird when he was on the corps until, until he retired that is." We stopped in front of a building at the mouth of the alleyway, right before going back out into the marketplace. Darius turned to me. "You are only a Private, that is the rank that everyone starts as. Even someone like Ed."

"What is that insignia?" I asked hoping it was something cool so I could impress Annabelle.

"Nothing." Darius said back. Once he saw my expression go from suspenseful excitement to slipping disappointment he began to laugh. "Your uniform will be plain for a while. Your first medals will be that of marksmanship, then the rest will be judged on your proficiency as an officer. However, rank advancement is slow."

"Why hold back the promotions?"

Darius grinned. "I asked something similar of Ed when I became a trooper. So I'll tell you what he told me. If everyone is a leader then who is there to follow? Barnaby, remember, the old must make way for the new."

"Is that why Ed retired?" I asked trying to understand what Darius meant.

"Making way for the future, passing the baton, retirement. Whatever you want to call it; I know Ed like no one else. He is like a father to me and he still has the same passion and energy for the job as he did when he was our age." Darius had passion for the man he called his mentor and the corps.

"Then why did he retire? You said it yourself he has the energy to do it, why not stick to it? Surely it's better than sitting in a barber shop." I pointed out.

"I don't know. He wouldn't give me a reason. But, best not to dwell on something that's not my business and not my place."

Darius turned and went into a building that was on the left. I followed Darius inside, there were four desks with various office supplies on them, but even with the stacks of paper they were still neat and orderly. Everything looked very professional. Light from the windows cast down upon the bookcases that held records of the town's history.

"This is our central headquarters. Now, you won't be in here unless instructed otherwise. Your job will be to patrol the streets within Gideon's borders to maintain peace and order. You will be given two uniforms, a name badge, and a firearm." Darius went over to the safe that was in the back of the room by a desk. He opened it and turned, showing me a small black gun. "Of course you won't be getting this until the recruiting process is over." Darius put the gun back into safe and locked it. Then he went over to the closet, opened the door and took out two green and black-accented uniforms. "You can go into the main office over there and change, I'll be right back—oh and don't touch anything." Darius departed and I was left standing there in the office. I walked into the side room like Darius said and changed.

The office was small; on the walls hung five pictures of different men. One of them was a younger Colonel Reynolds and another who stood out to me was a hardened-looking man, he looked like someone who would be in charge, who doesn't take nonsense. Was this the man who took over for Colonel Reynolds? On the desk was a large ornate map of the Confederate Conference of America; a small red dot marked where Gideon was located. The rest of the office wasn't much to take in, just books on shelves and a globe perched on a side table. My mind was on other things like my new job and my new home.

Just as I got into my new uniform there was a knock on the door. Darius was standing there holding out a small rectangle. "Here, take this", he said. I picked it up and held it in my hand, it was metal and had my last name on it: Maverick. "It is for your uniform, you are officially on patrol now." Darius smiled as I pinned it to my chest. "Now come on, we have to get going. We're already behind schedule."

We walked outside and into the marketplace. There was a lot of hustle and bustle and truth be told it was overwhelming. I saw Annabelle in the crowed buying some bread and my heart skipped a few beats. "Now, the thing to remember is to always stay vigilant and never stop taking in every detail. The people of Gideon are a good bunch, but they aren't the ones I worry about. Outsiders come through and think they are going to make off like bandits, but not on my watch. I suggest you adopt the same attitude." Darius kept peering through the crowed trying to find a needle in the haystack.

I, on the other hand, wasn't so focused. Everything to this point seemed like it moved too fast. I still felt as weak as I did when I collapsed in the streets of Ramsford, even though I now wore the uniform of an EBS Trooper. "All right, everything here seems to be in order." Darius scanned. Just as the words left his lips a woman came running up to us; she draped herself over me in a panic. "Officer Officer Theft at the church, the entire collection, gone!"

Darius turned to the women, "when?"

"Just now, he escaped on horse." She stammered over her words from worry. Darius took off in a run towards the direction of the crime, taking a moment to pry the woman off of me I sprinted to keep up. As we ran down the road towards the church Darius stopped and ran into a side door of a large building.

Before I could put much thought into his disappearance into the building, the large front doors flew open, and out came Darius holding the reins of two horses.

"Barnaby, come here now." Darius handed me the rein of one of the horses, the brown one with a white streak running down its face, Darius' horse was jet black and looked very majestic and powerful. He mounted the horse in one graceful motion and took off down the road without me. I had never ridden a horse before. It took a few tries to get up onto the saddle, but once I did get a good grasp on the reins and good foothold in the stirrup, the large and muscular beast took off. Pedestrians ducked out of the way as I flew through town hoping to catch up to both Darius and the thief. Passing the crowd that was gathered outside the church, I came to the outskirts of the town. It was beginning to turn into a more forested area, in the distance I saw Darius who was closing in on the man.

"Come on, let's get there first." I said to the horse, tapping my calves to its body. I wasn't sure if it was because I wanted to prove myself to everyone or that my adrenaline was the highest it had ever been, but I wasn't nervous at all and before long I had caught up to Darius who was fixed on capturing the thief.

An opening in the forest's path was coming up. It was a farm, with a rather high stone wall. The man and his horse cleared it without a problem.

"Ease off, Barnaby, we will find a way around." Darius called to me through the wind and galloping hooves.

"No way, he'll get away" I called back. Darius pulled his reins back and as he did he began to slow down. I knew that this was the moment where I go from zero to hero in Annabelle's eyes. With one hard kick my horse soared into the air and landed safely on the other side of the fence.

Stalks of wheat and corn hit my face as the chase continued. The man and his horse ducked into the barn that was located on the southern side of the farm. I came to a stop right outside knowing that entering on foot would be smarter. Quietly and cautiously I entered. His horse stood in the middle of the room eating some hay that had fallen onto the ground, it was just staring at me. The man though was nowhere to be found. I grew anxious, he could be anywhere, in the haystacks, in the rafters, in one of the many barrels.

I picked up a piece of wood that was leaning against one of the beams of the barn. Applying the advice Darius had given me in the marketplace I kept looking around and listening for anything and everything. Then I heard it. The small sound that a sword makes when it is being unsheathed filled the air behind me.

Turning around just in time the sword and wood I was holding clashed. Of course after a couple swings from the sword, the wood was sliced through completely and I was left defenseless. I ducked and grabbed a steel bucket that was on the ground next to a pile of hay and after dodging two more swings I managed to get the bucket over the man's head. He stumbled and fell into a trough of pig's feed. I picked up the sword just as he yanked the bucket off his head and pointed the blade close to his neck so he didn't dare move.

Darius ran through the door at the same moment. "Well, I see that you have the situation under control." He gave a hearty laugh. "Next time listen to your superiors," he paused, "but good work."

"No problem, so back to Gideon to give the collection back?" I asked feeling very accomplished.

"Yes, and then you can tell Annabelle." He smiled as my face turned red.

"What?" I stuttered

"I'm an officer of the law. I can read people. Don't worry, your secret is safe with me".

"Thanks," I sighed with relief.

"You'll earn that stripe soon enough." Darius grabbed the man and pulled him to his feet.

"What the hell is going on? Half my field is flattened by horse tracks and there is commotion in my barn." A thin elderly man stormed into the barn with a shotgun.

Darius held out his hand. "Hello sir, sorry about the mess. This man stole the collection from the church and we are just here to bring him to justice. If you would like we will replace any damaged crops and pay you for any damages done to the barn." Darius must deal with complaints often because this immediately calmed the man down.

"Stole from the church you say? Well, no replacement is necessary. I am happy that you caught him, officer." The man turned and left.

"That was nice of him." I was surprised the man didn't want some sort of payment for the damages to the field.

"Barnaby, you will find that the folks around here are good people and they appreciate that we are here to keep them safe. That is why when crooks like this come around they are happy to help in any way." Darius handcuffed the man.

The thief was bald and had white eyes. He was strong which was surprising because I managed to overcome him fairly easily. His face was calm for someone who was going to prison.

Darius tied the thief to the back of my horse, I rode upfront while Darius took up the rear so he could keep an eye on the man. It was a good day, I had gotten a great job in a great town, I even found my dream girl. My life was looking good. "Barnaby, look out!" That was all I heard before everything went dark.

I looked up into the white light. One by one bare tree

branches came into focus. I was laying flat on my back on the ground. Darius stood over me. "Are you all right?" He asked extending his hand to help me up.

"Yeah, I think so. My eye really hurts though. What happened?" I said, pulling myself up with Darius' help.

Darius looked at my eye that was quickly swelling. "Yeah, that is going to bruise, you'll be fine though. The thief was quick, he knocked you off your horse, mounted it and fled. But, we have the money, so it's okay, we will catch him another day." Darius was reassuring, yet the embarrassment of the thief's escape still lingered. "Now come on, we should return this to the preacher." The ride back was longer than I had remembered, maybe it was because we weren't moving at lighting speed or maybe it was because I was dreading returning as a defeated hero.

The crowd that had gathered outside the church during the robbery was long gone by now. In fact the streets of Gideon were quiet compared to the busy atmosphere of this morning. After tying the horse to a post, Darius knocked on the church's door and adjusted his uniform. I stood next to him holding my eye that had been bruised when I was knocked off the horse.

The door creaked open and there stood a slender man, his hair was black with streaks of white. He was well groomed and had a nice, welcoming smile. His eyes were like two pieces of coal. His black pants and black shirt where worn under a black long coat.

"You don't have to knock to gain entrance to God's

house." His voice was that of a gentleman's; it was clear, charismatic and well educated. "Come in, come in." The Preacher ushered us in. The church was small, with just four pews on each side, it made for an intimate atmosphere. There was a simple marble top table on the altar and candles dotted the room like glowing stars of the night. "Sorry about all the commotion this morning, officers. It is a shame that a man would think he has to steal to get what he wants. Unfortunately, there are those who feel backed into a corner." The Preacher didn't sound mad, he sounded sorry for the thief.

"Yes, but the law cannot take pity even for those who choose the wrong path." Darius was less willing to let this go.

We entered the side room of the church. There was a picture hung of Jesus Christ behind the desk. The Preacher offered us the two seats that faced the desk while he took the one on the other side. "So, you have him in custody then? When will he be tried? I want to help in his defense." The Preacher was determined to help this man even though he wronged the church.

"As of now, he is still at large somewhere in the backwoods of Gideon, however we were able to recover the stolen money." Darius reported.

"Oh good, no harm done. It is best to leave muddy water to settle. No need to go looking for trouble when there is none to be found. Let him go." The Preacher said.

"That idea would be taken into consideration if he didn't assault an officer and take one of our horses. Taking the amount of money he did from today's collection is considered a petty theft in the eyes of our department. A whole horse, on the other hand is a different story and assaulting an officer is more than enough to issue a warrant." Darius spoke as if he was reading from a law book. The Preacher lowered his head and shook it, he looked disappointed.

"Preacher, sometimes we must help those who have strayed, even if they don't want us to. And even if how we help them is not in their favor." The Preacher lifted his head and looked at me.

"Son, you are right. But, it is the choices we make that will be remembered, not the laws that guided our hand."

Darius put the small bag of coins onto the Preacher's desk. "Preacher, it has been a pleasure. I will send two officers over in the morning for an official report on what happened. Please be cooperative in our investigation." Darius stood up.

"May I have a second?" The Preacher gestured to me.

"Yes, but make it quick. I will be outside." When Darius left the room the tension settled but there was still a residue of something left unsaid. I haven't been in a church for a while and the last time I was in one it wasn't a fond memory.

"Do you know who came to this house yesterday, son?" He asked me.

"No?" Did this have something to do with the robbery?

"God," the Preacher sounded excited but I didn't know what he meant by that. Since this is a church isn't God always present?

"That's nice." I tried to go a long with it. My faith wasn't all that strong even after my conversation with Neo so it was hard to be as excited as the Preacher, I just didn't believe.

"God came down to me in one of his many forms and knocked on the very same door you entered through today. That's right, God knocked on his own home. He bore a message son, a message I was told to deliver to you."

"How do you know He wanted the message delivered to me?" The Preacher was obviously mistaken.

"Your name is Barnaby, isn't it?" The Preacher asked.

"Well, yeah but-" I stuttered.

The Preacher smiled once again. "I told you, the Lord came to me last night and told me this would happen. He said 'the final reckoning will come, follow with trust my second-born son.' Then, He left."

"I am not sure I understand," I admitted.

"You see, it is not about a thief who steals from the church; it is about the events that follow. You were meant to return the stolen money so I could deliver this message to you."

"Couldn't the theft have been avoided? I am sure there could have been another way to deliver the message. You have to admit this has become quite the inconvenience for both the department and for the people who work hard so that they can donate each week."

"I know, but remember, Barnaby, God doesn't always

work in ways which we would like. He does what is best for us, what is best for the collective whole." The Preacher looked to the picture, then to me. "I wonder what he meant by 'the final reckoning will come, follow with trust my second born son.' What do you think he has in store?"

"I honestly have no idea, I am sorry." I still wasn't one hundred percent believing that God came to the Preacher, it could have been a silly prank.

"Well, I am sure we will soon find out won't we?" The Preacher sighed.

"What exactly are you saying?" I was still trying to comprehend

"I am not saying anything, God is"

I stood up, "it's been nice talking to you, but I have to leave now."

"I understand, but before you go take into consideration these words: as we run away from the destiny set forth in front of us, we often at times find that we stumble upon that very destiny faced with an unfavorable hand."

Catching up to Darius I could tell instantly that he was frustrated. A combination of not catching the crook and not getting the feedback from the Preacher he expected was probably the cause. I decided it was best not to tell him what the Preacher told me. It would probably cause him to explode.

"It isn't that I blame you," Darius began, "it is the fact that the Preacher is being blind to the whole situation."

"What is he not seeing?" I asked, trying to not be blind myself.

"He doesn't realize, people like that are like hungry wolves. You let them into the flock once and over time they devour the whole heard." Darius was sure that the man would be back and now I was starting to feel the same.

It was dusk when we arrived back at the inn. "All right, I will see you tomorrow bright and early. In the mean time I will tell the night guard to keep an eye on the Preacher."

"Why? Is he a suspect?" I asked, I certainly was still trying to figure out who the Preacher was exactly.

"No, I just don't want him screwing with the investigation. Anyway Barnaby, see you tomorrow, goodnight." Darius turned and began walking away.

"Goodnight Darius," I called.

I entered the pub at the inn. It was the same scene as the previous night. Annabelle was behind the bar serving drinks, I sat at a table near the fire to warm up, it had been a long day. My eye was sore and I felt like there was a ton of bricks stacked on my chest.

"Looks like you had a rough day." Annabelle's voice felt like a soothing chime in the soft breeze of spring.

"It is all in a days work. After all I am a Trooper now." I tried to act as if my bruised face and weathered look were nothing more then a normal occurrence.

"Yeah, you look like you really know what you're doing."

She rolled her eyes and handed me a cup of warm tea.

Sitting up in the chair I decided to tell her about my dangerous apprehension of the thief that stole from the church. That would have to impress her. "You should have seen me today, there was a horse chase and then I had to fight an armed bandit with nothing but a piece of scrap wood." I sipped the tea impressed with myself.

"Is that where you got the black eye?" She smirked and let out a small laugh. "Don't get cocky now, remember you have to earn those stripes, boy." She turned around and started to walk back to the bar. My cheeks felt warm and I knew that she saw me blush. I sat there and finished my tea before retiring to bed for the night.

— Chapter Four —

Battle of Gideon

I sat up, looking around at the bodies lying in the field around me. Where was I? The sky was swirling with a mixture of red and bright thunderous light. Everything was still, silent, untouched by time and the reality of space. This was another dimension, a place in which peace no longer existed. Fires burned the ground and what wasn't burning was left wilted and black. I stood up, hearing shouts and screams miles away. Had the battle moved on? Who was fighting and why?

I stood atop a hill looking down into a valley, there rested a small ruin in the center. Beyond that I saw a black hillside, it must have been less than a mile away but it felt like it was on the other end of the world. I turned to my right and saw a large building with high walls around it. The reflecting power of the golden pillars and the golden roof blinded me as I gazed upon its odd placement, perched above all the destruction.

Wind whipped across my face as a ripping sound filled the air. Looking to the sky, I saw the clouds part in a most ferocious and violent way. Pure light came forth to the structure from up above and danced around surrounding it in a veil. Brick by brick, one by one, the building broke apart and rose up through the surrounding black skies. The bright spectacle was unfurling as I stood, frozen and bewildered, unable to move or turn away. When the last of the stone and gold ornate cap disappeared into the sky, there was silence, no visual evidence to say the grandiose building was ever there, not even a hole in the ground to mark its foundation could be spoken of. All that was left was silence.

"Hello?" A voice called through the thick air. I turned in a panic, for it was not what I expected to hear especially since I was standing in a field of motionless, lifeless bodies.

Before me stood a man holding a sword he was wounded in several places. He had a goatee and his purple eyes were filled with tears. His dark skin blended with his brown hair.

"Hello," I simply answered, not knowing what to do.

"You can see me? You can hear me?" He turned his head slightly as he questioned the possibility of my existence.

"Yes?" As if the bodies and the disappearing buildings weren't enough, now I was face to face with an armed stranger who was giving off a crazy vibe.

"By grace, is this possible?" The man was starting to freak me out, we were both in the middle of nowhere and he was covered in either his or someone else's blood.

"It seems so." I slowly responded taking a few steps back. I wanted to get away from this man.

"You must come with me, hurry. We must move quickly before they return. I will explain, or rather He will explain when we get there." Before I could get away he grabbed my wrist and brought me a short distance away from the valley. He stopped, looked around and knelt down.

Considering he was armed and I wasn't, I knew I wasn't going anywhere. The man lifted a trap door of some kind, it revealed a staircase that led to a hallway made of stone. "Quickly, time is of the essence." He said in a hushed whisper.

Reluctantly I walked down the stairs and down through the hallway. The man followed and lit a torch that hung at the bottom of the stairs. "Come now with me." He continued leading the way. In less then two hundred feet we came to a solid wooden door. The man turned to me and smiled.

"Hello Barnaby. We have been waiting for you. My name is Angelo."

"How do you know my name? What happened? Where are we? What is this?" My questions came through as jumbled words as I stood there in the dimly lit hall.

"All questions will be answered in time. Just know that you are safe here. Hope has risen, prayer has proved to prosper and prophecy is about to unfold. The age of resolution through revelation has begun. Thanks to you." Angelo turned and opened the door, light poured in; he

walked through and I followed.

"Barnaby! Barnaby! Let's go!" Darius shouted as I woke. He was standing in the doorway holding two rifles.

"What's going on?" I asked, standing up in just a white shirt and pajama bottoms.

"I don't know. Looters, raiders, could be a war tribe by the looks of the damage they are doing. It's time to earn that marksmanship, buddy." Darius tossed me one of the rifles, it was clunky and heavy in my hands. "Now get ready and get downstairs. The Troopers are assembling by the market; it's time to push them back."

Darius ran down the hall. Wasting no time I jumped into my uniform and bolted after him rifle in hand. I arrived at the marketplace no less than three minutes later. All members of the EBS Trooper Corps were present. Some townspeople also were gathered, some of them setting up a field hospital and others were arming themselves. It was a sight to behold, the chill of the night air slapped my face as I looked for Darius for my orders.

"Darius!" I called over the commotion.

"Barnaby!" Darius swiftly approached me. "The commander is on his way, this is going to get heavy, I want you to stay with the reserves." Darius didn't sound nervous at all, although he was well aware of the gravity of the situation.

"No, this is my town as much as it is yours. I am staying in the front to fight." Even though I could tell he did not like the idea, he couldn't stop me from meeting the enemy head on. After all the commander would need all guns and manpower to hold back the advancing threat.

"Fine, but stay close to me." We made our way to the front of the line. The commander of Gideon rode up on a gold steed. His uniform was the same as the one Colonel Reynolds had hanging in his shop, blue with black leather trim. Four rows of medals lined his chest.

"Soldiers and citizens of Gideon." A silence filled the air, but the sound of the enclosing force was growing louder. "Orders are simple, Troopers do not give an inch, auxiliary will replace wounded Troopers but everyone goes home tonight, understand? Darius, you take charge as line commander, on your order." Darius nodded to the commanding officer.

"He isn't staying up here with us?" I asked confused and concerned.

"He would be too easy of a target on top of that horse, he will direct the movement of ranks throughout the battle from behind. My job is just to maintain the formation of the firing line. Keep an ear out for the orders."

"What are they?" I asked yet again out of curiosity and concern.

"Fire and brace." He exclaimed.

"I know what fire means, just remind me again what brace entails?" I suddenly realized I was very inexperienced in this form of fighting and Darius' caution should have been considered.

"It means brace yourself for the enemy. It is given when

the enemy charges into the line. That is the point in battle where the line is at its most critical to fail." Darius said this as if it was common knowledge.

Now I was certain I should have taken Darius' advice. Compared to everyone else in the formation, I would be the crack in the dam.

Swallowing my doubt, I filled my thoughts with other things. I began to think of what lay beyond us; the other half of the town was falling to the enemy and I don't know what was harder for everyone in the marketplace to contemplate—their fellow citizens perishing in the flames that kept sprouting up from the other side of town, or the agonizing anticipation of guessing the strength and numbers the enemy force possessed. You couldn't help but hold your breath over the next few moments.

The opposition emerged into the square from the smoke and the shadows of the buildings. They wore black hoods with various weapons in hand such as bats and swords and, as I feared, they outnumbered us. They stopped about a dozen yards away and it became a standoff; they stood on one side and we the other. One man came forward and removed his hood. With jet-black hair and a grim disposition, he introduced himself. "My name is Cain. Lay down your arms and you'll die swiftly." Cain unsheathed his sword and flashed a wicked grin.

"Ready, aim!" Darius called. The entire line aimed their rifles ahead. Bringing the butt of my rifle to my shoulder, I looked down the sights choosing a target. "On my command."

Darius aimed his rifle.

"Never easy," chuckled Cain. The mob ran for the line of Troopers, battle cries and raised weaponry were closing in.

"Fire!" Darius screamed. A barrage of bullets ripped through the enemy force. Dozens fell, but the crowd kept coming. "Fire " Darius called once more. I pulled open the bolt letting out the used cartridge, my hands shaking from nerves, but I knew I had a job to do. Closing the bolt I prepared to fire again. The mob wasn't slowing down and their numbers didn't seem to dwindle in the barrage of fire.

"Brace!" Darius shouted over gun smoke and flash. Before the initial shock of being slammed into the ground was realized, I found myself facing upward, looking at the night sky. Figures rushed past me as battle cries mixed together with the sounds of gunfire, creating a swirl of confusion within the ranks. Using my rifle as a crutch I pulled myself back onto my feet. Formation was impossible to hold and rifles were replaced by swords and fists. It was bloody, barbaric, and unpredictable in the sense of which side was winning. I reloaded my rifle once more, looking around to try and see if I could find Darius.

An unknown man came charging at me with a club. He was only a few feet away before I pulled the trigger, blasting him backwards and onto his back. I tried to reload, however the bolt was caught. The intensity of the battle growing I had no other choice, I had to find Darius. "Darius, Darius!" I yelled throwing my rifle to the ground. Moments passed, "Darius, where are you?"

"I'm here!" Darius cut through the crowed with the blade of his sword. "Go to the inn and wait for me there."

"I'm not going to leave," I argued.

"Go!" he shoved me in the direction of the inn.

I pushed my way through the bloody market square and back up the street to the inn, it was dark and the inn looked ransacked and deserted. "Darius is going to meet me here." I assured myself. "Stay calm and wait for him here."

"Down now." The door of the inn swung open and Annabelle came forth, shotgun in hand.

"Don't shoot " I threw myself on the ground. Two loud bangs rocketed through the air.

"You look stupid, get up," she said once the noise subsided.

Looking behind me I saw two of the aggressors from the square lying motionless; they must have followed me. "You saved me?" I said in shock.

"Yes, I saved you. You know, I never saw a Trooper cower like that." My face began to blush. "Don't worry I won't tell anyone," she said. "Now come inside."

I didn't have to be told twice. I got up and ran for the door. Once inside, Annabelle went back behind the bar and poured two drinks from a barrel. "Here. Drink this, you're shaking, it will calm your nerves."

The intensity of being in battle for the first time shook me to the core. Minutes seemed like hours as we sat there in silence waiting for Darius to return.

Even with everything going on outside I couldn't help but notice how beautiful Annabelle truly was. The candle light illuminated her clear and smooth skin in the darkness. "Hey Annabelle," I began to say.

"What?" she said, loading the shotgun she had fired previously.

"In case we die, I wanted you to know." I cleared my throat.

Annabelle closed the breach making it ready to fire, I gulped. Then she looked at me. "You were saying?"

"Uh…" after careful consideration I decided it was best not to say anything.

Luckily there was a loud bang on the door to break the awaked tension. However, with the noise came a draining feeling of fear. What or who made the noise? Annabelle took the shotgun and pointed it toward the door. "Get behind me." She said blowing a strand of hair out of her face.

"Its me, Darius." Without thinking I ran past Annabelle and opened the door. In stumbled Darius who was wounded in the arm. I closed the door behind him while Annabelle brought over a chair then ran behind the bar.

"Are you okay?" I asked.

"Yes I am fine, but Gideon has fallen. Shortly after you left something happened."

"Here." Annabelle came over to Darius and began to clean

his arm wound with water.

"What happened?" I asked.

"We thought we had them beat and then something started happening to them. Their skin started turning rough and scaly like reptiles, and their teeth were sharp and crude."

"You must have been imagining things." Annabelle said as she began wrapping his arm with a bandage.

"No I wasn't, they tore through who was left like we were nothing more than tissue paper. The commander disappeared in the chaos and the line collapsed. It was horrid." Darius for the first time looked like he was in shock.

"What do we do?" I asked.

Darius looked at me, his expression changed to one of responsibility. "We go find Colonel Reynolds, he will know what to do."

"Okay I just have to grab something from upstairs and then we can go."

"What is it?" Annabelle spat.

"It is just important, it was given to me by a friend." I answered.

Annabelle rolled her eyes. "Fine, but hurry—we don't have the comfort of time." Wasting no time, I ran for the stairs.

Swinging open the door I grabbed my backpack and flung it over my shoulders. I looked out the window that looked over the entire town. The glow from the fire engulfed Gideon.

It wasn't the town burning or the people being chased

down to their deaths that disturbed me, it was what was chasing them. Just as Darius had described there were these lizard-man beings. They were superhuman in size, with giant muscles and giant wings protruding out of their shoulder blades. I looked at the sky that was forming over Gideon—it seemed like it was churning just like the sky in my dream. What was going on? None of this made sense.

Wood and glass shattered as one of the reptilian figures crashed through the wall. It roared and bared its crooked, jagged teeth. Its yellows eyes were fixated on me as it hunched its back and flexed its body. I slowly backed up as it stomped the ground shaking the entire room. Flaring its nostrils, it cornered me against a wall. Then it smiled and slowly, in one motion the creature changed its form. It became Cain.

"What do you want?" I said shaking, not believing my eyes.

"What, no hello?" He laughed. "I thought the great Barnaby would be...well let's just say you aren't what I expected." His smile was wicked and cruel; blood and dirt stained his teeth.

"How do you know my name?" I demanded.

He chuckled like what I said was a joke. "Everyone knows your name. Why do you think we are here?" Cain drew a sword that rested in a hilt on his hip and pointed it directly at me. "Now come with me."

A sound came from inside my backpack.

"What is that?" Cain said with anger.

"Its just my backpack," I answered, secretly wanting to know what was making the noise as well.

"Open it." He said, still pointing the sword at me.

"You open it." I wasn't about to take orders from this creep.

"Give it to me then." He spat. Reluctantly, I took the pack off and threw it onto the ground in front of him. As the pack lay on the ground it began to move rapidly, it started to move around the floor; was there something trapped in there?

"I don't have time for this, enough." Cain stabbed the bag pinning it to the ground. The motion stopped. "Good, now that that's settled." He drew his attention back to me, but when he did, he didn't notice the bag wiggle.

"How do you know me?" I said quickly, still eyeing the bag.

"I come from a place that is said to be legend and in this place you are the root of legend." He moved another step closer.

"And what does this legend pertain to exactly?" I said trying to buy just a smidgen more time so I could find out what was in the bag.

Cain stopped his advance. "What we have all been waiting for."

"And that is?" I asked.

Cain held out his arms like he was a ringmaster addressing a large crowd, he was quiet hysterical with joy. "For the finale to the struggle that never ends." Cain raised his sword to my neck.

"Now come with me. There is someone who wants desperately to meet you."

Were my eyes deceiving me? It seemed that everything that I knew of reality was collapsing around me. Rising from behind Cain grew a monstrous grey beast that rivaled the form in which Cain appeared. A stone mane with two horns jutted out from its head. It snarled and flashed two teeth that were at least a half a foot long. Slowly Cain turned around and faced the creature.

"I am Elek, the protector." The creature spoke in a low, ancient tone. It was the gargoyle that Neo had given to me on the train.

In a flash Cain took the form of the terrible reptile again, and letting out a ear-piercing shriek he lunged for Elek. The two met with a bang. They began clawing and biting each other, slamming each other against the remaining walls of the room. Elek was superior in size, strength, and ability and he quickly overpowered Cain. Just as the fight was drawing to the final blow, Cain sprouted wings and flew out into the night sky. As he left, Elek let out a magnificent roar that sent a shiver down my spine. Though Elek had saved my life, I stood frozen, unable to move and breathe.

Elek turned back to me. "Do not fear. I am Elek, the protector."

"Yeah, I got that part." I said in a shaky voice. "But why are you here?"

"I am called when my master beckons." Elek said as he

knelt down on one knee and placed his fist over his chest.

I went from completely terrified to very confused. None of this added up to much other than the fact that I was almost killed by one mysterious beast and then saved by another. "You can get off the ground, Elek," I said.

Elek stood up and looked at me. We both faced each other in silence.

"So, you say your master beckoned you?" I asked, I was more comfortable than I should have been with the fact that Elek went from a pocket-sized knick-knack to a larger-than-life "protector" of some kind.

"Yes, I am Elek, the protector."

"I know that. But, **why** are you here? What are you protecting me from?"

"Soon."

"What's that supposed to mean? Why won't you tell me?" What was so important that it would have to wait for me to hear?.

"Until the time comes," he uttered.

"Barnaby, open this door now " I heard the voices of Annabelle and Darius from outside the door.

"One second," I said turing to the door. I had more questions for Elek, but when I turned back he had returned to his smaller form. I picked him up and put him in my pack.

Bang! Annabelle shot the hinge of the door blasting it open. "What the hell did you do to the place?" Annabelle asked, looking at the giant hole in the side of the wall.

"We have no time to discuss this," Darius interrupted. "Colonel Reynolds is expecting us." Slinging the backpack over my shoulders, I followed them out the door.

Chapter Five

The Serpent's Bloody Cross

Making our way through the back alleys of what was left of Gideon, we came to a series of small houses. The entire time I was thinking of Cain's words. I began to think of the Preacher's words as well—what the hell was going on? We arrived within minutes. The door to Colonel Reynolds' house was open. With pistol in hand Darius led Annabelle and I into the house.

"Hello? Sir, are you here?" Darius said softly but firmly, low moans came from inside. We rushed into the parlor and saw Mrs. Reynolds in a pool of her own blood, cradled by Ed.

"What happened?" Darius asked, lowering his pistol and running over to them. Annabelle ran to the drapes and pulled them from the window. She ran over to Mrs. Reynolds and held them against the large wound. She was covered in blood from her silver hair to her tan slippers.

Mr. Reynolds was shaken and could barley speak. "These fellas came in and attacked my wife. I managed to fight them off but not before they did this to her." Ed looked down to his injured love.

"We are here to help, don't worry." I assured.

"Do you know what they could have wanted?" There was such a mixture of confusion and pain in Ed's voice.

"We will find out, I promise." I kept trying to reassure Mr.

Reynolds that he wasn't alone in this situation and that we were going to get to the bottom of this.

"Barnaby, come here." Darius was focused.

"Yes?" I said crossing the room.

"I want you to cover the rest of us, all right?" Darius looked me straight in the eye as he said this. "I am going to see if we can get to the doctor's down the road."

"Son," called Mr. Reynolds. I turned around, "upstairs is where I have my rifle. Go and get it, you can use that." He turned to Darius. "Get her out of here."

I ran upstairs. There were only two small rooms, so finding the rifle didn't take much time. I loaded five rounds and closed the bolt, then stuffed a handful of bullets into my pocket. By the time I got downstairs they were ready to move. No time would be wasted. We went out the back door and back into the maze of alley ways. We would have to head back toward the marketplace; gun shots could still be heard in the close distance. The smoky air didn't allow for deep breaths and the fire heated the cool air of the winter's night.

"Okay, we move as one and we move slowly." Darius whispered. He took point as I stayed back to cover the rear. Practically crawling through the twisting alleys, Mrs. Reynolds' condition worsened. "Almost there." Darius said "Hold on, everyone."

Coming to a dead stop I bumped into Annabelle. "Watch it," she hissed, nudging me.

"Sorry," I whispered back.

"Okay this is going to be tricky. They set up some sort of encampment in the market square and we have to cross it." I could tell that Darius' mind was applying all his tactical training to try and solve this problem

Suddenly, and without a word Darius left us crouching behind one of the buildings that lined the square. I was not ready for him to leave. I needed Darius to show me the way, I needed him to teach me.

Those gathered in the square suddenly stopped mingling as if they all sensed something at the same time. The galloping of a horse sounded through the square, Darius astride. The startled crowd took chase and soon the square was empty.

"He bought us time, now go!" Mr. Reynolds was thankful, and was filled with pride.

After reaching the doctor's office we laid Mrs. Reynolds on the examination table. None of the staff was present and between the three of us we had little medical knowledge. Annabelle didn't let that stop her as she took charge of the room, as she began getting Mrs. Reynolds comfortable.

"Well?" said a hopeful Mr. Reynolds.

"She lost a lot of blood and she is very weak. Only time will tell." Annabelle said.

"We don't have time, when will she be okay? I know a place a few miles down the road, a good friend lives there. Can she be loaded onto a wagon?" Ed asked.

"No, she will have to rest for the night." Annabelle said gently, she turned to me. "Better get ready with that thing. You'll need it if they find out where we are."

I stood by the door of the office looking through the small window. The square started to fill up again with people or whatever they were. Does this mean that they gave up on the chase? Or did they catch up with Darius?

I pushed the thought from my mind. As soon as I did this however another thought moved its way in. Ed Reynolds loved nothing more in this world than his wife and she was dying. It reminded me of when I lost my family. One by one I saw them leave me and one by one they took a piece of me with them. Now, as I feared, I am feeling them leave me all over again.

"Everything look okay out there?" Annabelle's voice sounded so sweet but I hardly noticed her as I slipped into a dark and lonely feeling.

"Yeah." I answered coldly, not turning around. I felt myself being sucked back into the depression that nearly took my life as it did my father's and mother's. My mind replayed a memory that I had all but forgotten, or so I thought.

It was the end of spring and the summer air was moving in. Naturally it was warm and sunny; the blue sky and slight breeze brought much joy, but not for me. One week prior my father had drunk his last bottle and my mother had passed three days before that. I was the only one left who could feel the pain. I found myself standing right at

the edge of the very place where my brother stood before he plunged into the existence of my memories. Looking down, then up I saw a single white cloud pass by. "You did this, You did all of this." I remember saying this as if the cloud was God himself. My breathing was steady and my heartbeat heavy and slow. I closed my eyes. I was ready.

Breaking the rhythm of the swirling air came a tiny hoot. I looked around for the sound and there perched on the roof was a small brown owl with beady eyes. It looked up at me and turned its head slightly from left to right as it sang. I looked back to the ground, ignoring the owl as I prepared myself for the final leap.

I could hear the hooting and chirping of the owl as it tried to get my attention.

The owl was acting extremely strange, maybe he sensed the end? My mom always told me there was a instinct in all living things that linked everything together, that everything had a basic understanding of life and the unfortunate event of death.

"Greet me at the gates, okay?" I said under my breath closing my eyes and taking a step toward the edge. A single tear started to slide down my cheek.

I felt something small flutter past my ear and land on my shoulder, opening my eyes yet again I saw that the tiny owl was now perched upon my shoulder. "Yes?" I asked it. It hooted as if to respond.

"I have to, it will cease the pain." I argued trying to convince myself. The owl hooted twice and I found myself in conversation.

"Thanks for the concern, I think?" I couldn't understand him or why he was hooting at me, but he was distracting me from the task at hand and I had to end this so I could finally be with my family once and forever.

I took the owl in the palm of my hand and turned around to place it back onto the roof. As I tried to shake it from my hand it began to squawk and flap frantically. I soon found out why.

The church had a fireplace to keep the parishioners warm in the winter. The chimney stuck out in the middle of the roof around the church. There, coiled around the chimney, was a nasty black snake with yellow eyes. A red stripe along the length of its body fanned out on its head in the shape of what looked like a bloody cross. I had never seen a snake in person before. Many reptiles died out during the war and never returned when other life did, but even so I had a feeling that something was peculiar about this one.

Flying from my hand, the tiny owl attacked the snake. Pecking and dodging the snake's mouth, it hooted and flew in a frenzy. The snake grew more and more frustrated as the bird began to draw blood from its side. However, with one quick flick of the snake's tail, the bird fell to the ground.

Returning its attention to me, the snake slithered

down from the chimney and approached. In a terrifying pose the snake curled up and pointed itself at me, ready to strike. Suddenly, I felt that I did not want to die. Panicking, I had no where to run. I was backed up to the edge of the roof. "Help!"

Dodging feathers and bloody scales I leaped out of the way, a larger bird appeared from thin air. The two animals tumbled off the roof's edge and down to the gravel below. Moments passed, and as I laid on the roof thanking everything and everyone for saving my skin, I kept my gaze to where the two animals disappeared. As the moments turned to minutes, one flap filled the air and then another. Rising up and then landing on the building was an eagle, the bird that had fought with the snake.

It was bold and fierce, very commanding, wise and elegant, a creature that demanded respect and was naturally given it. It was brown with magnificent blue stormy eyes and a golden beak. We studied each other. Its bloody talons and beak were marks of a victor. "Thank you," I said, though I knew it couldn't understand me.

The eagle walked over to the small owl that gave its life to save me from the snake. It lowered its beak to the motionless body. "Hey! Get away from him, you can't have him, he helped me."

I stood up and ran over. "I said go away, he saved me and I won't have you eat him." I tried to shoo the eagle away but he was too quick. He cradled the little owl in one of his talons and took off like lighting into the sky. "Hey! I said don't..."

Who was I kidding? It was the way of nature; like my family, I wasn't ready to let the bird go either. The sadness and pain came back but I didn't plan on jumping this time. The little owl gave its own life, so I would do as it would have wanted me to—and that was to live.

"Hey, hey, hello? Barnaby." Annabelle nudged me back into focus. I cleared the thought from my mind, pushing it back into my subconscious. "Are you okay?"

"Yeah, I am fine. What's up?" I asked trying to get off the subject.

"We need help moving Mrs. Reynolds into the cellar. We are all too tired to stay up and Mr. Reynolds and I both agreed that it would be safer to be in the cellar than on the main floor where those creeps can find us."

"Yeah, I agree." Getting Mrs. Reynolds settled was difficult. She wasn't bleeding anymore, but she wasn't able to move by herself at all. She was very delicate and the stairs to the cellar of the doctor's office were narrow. But finally, after about an hour, we were all settled in. Mrs. Reynolds was placed on a table downstairs and given most of the blankets. Mr. Reynolds pulled up a chair and slept with his head on the tabletop beside her and I found a spot near a cabinet filled with medications.

"Barnaby," a soft voice filled the silent air.

"Annabelle?" I asked trying to make out the figure in the dark.

"Would you mind if I slept next to you? It's freezing." She asked.

I couldn't believe it. *Say something!* I said to myself. "Uh-", but before I could get anything out she laid down next to me. "Uh, sure." I stammered.

"You know, I just wanted to say that I think you are a nice guy, even though you can be clumsy," she said, turning to me. Our faces were only inches apart.

"Yeah, you're pretty cool too." I wasn't smooth at all and I think she could tell. She smiled softly and blinked slowly. "Well, goodnight." I turned around fearing that even though it was dark, she would still see me blushing.

"Goodnight?" She sounded disappointed and I immediately regretted ending our conversation. This was the first time that I might have actually had the chance to talk to her, one on one on such an intimate level. However, even though I wanted to turn back around and say something to her, I gave in to a much needed sleep.

— Chapter Six —
Meeting the Family

"Wake up, you're drooling." I picked my head up and looked around. That didn't sound like Annabelle's voice.

A man was looking at me from across the table. He had white hair and blue eyes, brown stubble, and looked annoyed. Was I going crazy? Were these dreams a recurring plot to my decaying reality?

"Sorry," I said wiping my lip.

"It's okay, dear." A women's voice answered. I looked at her and she smiled. She had white hair with golden leaves placed gently within the strands. Her violet eyes sparkled in the glowing candle that illuminated her pale, smooth skin.

"Can someone please tell me what is going on?" I begged.

"Sorry kid, that is going to have to wait; in the meantime just come up with something and hold onto it as your reality, considering yours is falling apart."

"Enough of that." The women said to the man. She turned back to me. "Forgive him, it is not our place to tell you what you wish to know."

"It is not his place to be here." The man had some beef with me and I didn't have the slightest clue why.

"Listen, I have no idea why I am here and why

everyone seems to know who I am, so cut me some slack. You think I want to be here?" I snapped back.

"All right, that is enough, you two." There was another voice from behind a wooden door. It was older and the others seemed to react to it with much respect and love. The presence of something great, something warm and peaceful filled the small, dimly lit room. It was like royalty sweeping into a tiny peasant village.

The Man entered through the door that Angelo led me through in my previous dream. However, when the Man entered the room, He didn't look like what I had expected. The anticipation of his arrival was immense—as vast as the night sky and as mysterious as the shadows that haunted my dreams. But when He entered, He was more or less just like any other man.

A plain hooded cloak reached His ankles. His shirt was tan and his cloak was a light brown, and a dark brown fabric belt was tied around His waist. His wavy hair was a rich grey and his smile was welcoming in every sense of the word. His stormy blue eyes had a mixture of golden swirling flakes that reflected light ever so slightly.

"Hello, Barnaby." His tone was friendly, like we had known each other forever.

"Why does everyone know my name?" I bursted.

He took a seat. "You're safe here and all your questions will be answered in time," the older Man said.

"Everyone keeps saying that too. What is going on?" I was borderline hysterical.

"I am sorry, you are right; it isn't right for us to know who you are and for you to be left in the dark. Barnaby, I am God."

"Yeah, sure you are." I said looking back at him with doubt.

"We understand why you would say that." the woman tried to comfort me. "But, know we are who we say we are."

"Who are you then?" I asked, not believing her either.

"I am Fay, the angel of faith." Fay introduced herself with a smile. She was quite pretty.

"And you?" I said looking to the man who was more or less annoyed with this entire situation.

"I'm Michael," he said.

"I'm sorry—who?" I decided to have a little fun with him.

"Michael? The Archangel?" he was growing more and more frustrated with me.

"Never heard of you." I shrugged and both God and Fay let out a small smile. Michael was not so enthused. He turned to God.

"Really? You couldn't get someone who at least knew and appreciated the immensity of this crisis?"

"We will fill him in, he will be fine." God assured.

"So you guys are angels?" I asked.

"Yes," Fay answered sweetly.

"Are there many more of you?" I asked.

"There were, and there still would be if things would have gone differently." Michael said in a snarky manner.

"What's done is done and if it is to be undone, then we must learn to walk again so we may soon come to run." God looked to me. "We don't have much time to talk now, Barnaby. Just know that someday we will. As for right now, all I want you to do is use your best judgment and be open to the signs and gifts that you have been given, for they are your armament. With these tools you will lead the rebellion against Lucifer."

"Excuse me?" My mouth almost feel open, "you want me to do what?

God smiled. "That is all that can be said at this moment. Remember, sometimes knowing someone is out there looking after you is enough to ignite the best." The room faded to black.

I woke. Annabelle was leaning over me in the makeshift bed that I had made. Tears streaked her face.

"Whats the matter?" I asked, still trying to wrap my head around whether or not that dream was actually real or just my imagination.

"Mrs. Reynolds didn't make it through the night." She barely got the sentence out.

"How is Mr. Reynolds?" I asked solemnly.

"He is okay, he told me he knew from the moment it happened." She sat up.

Sitting up, I rubbed my eyes, "Annabelle, I know this is hard to think about considering what happened, but what is our next move? We have to leave Gideon—it's not safe."

"I know. I checked to see if the coast was clear this morning and the square was still filled up. Seems like they are looking for something, they keep sending patrols out." She and I both stood up. I could see Mr. Reynolds next to the table of the still Mrs. Reynolds. The desolate sound of sobbing was heard.

"I think I know what is happening," I said, thinking back to everything that had happened. I felt unbearable guilt that somehow I was the cause of all this, and it was continuing to grow more dangerous for those around me by each passing moment.

"What?" Annabelle looked at me.

"I can't fully explain now, it is hard enough for me to believe it myself. But, we need to find the Preacher, if he is still out there." I hoped he was. If everything I had experienced was reality and not just part of my imagination, then the Preacher would be the only other person I knew who would believe me without doubt.

"Barnaby, I am not sure the church is even still standing, the entire town was up in flames," she tried to explain.

"I know, but maybe, just maybe by the grace of God he is alive. That he got out in time and managed to stay hidden like we have. We need to try to find him, Annabelle, trust me on this one," I said looking directly into her eyes.

She was beautiful even in the presence of death. Amidst the destruction and inexplicable chaos, she was the diamond in a dark mine. She looked at me with a peculiar stare; I had changed since we'd first met. She had seen me as weak and wounded, although now I was taking charge to help the situation for the good. Maybe there was a leader in me after all.

"All right, but you go and find the Preacher on your own. I will stay behind with Mr. Reynolds, when you return we'll leave," she said, putting back up her defenses.

"Okay, that is fine. After all we don't know how dangerous it is out there." I said, trying to maintain my new sense of leadership.

"I can handle myself," she shot me with dagger eyes.

I had blown it. I went upstairs silently, tail tucked between my legs. I walked slowly and quietly up to the window. Looking out I saw exactly what Annabelle had described. There were around twenty people left in the square. They looked dirty and rotten, and I was convinced now that they could all turn into those reptilian freaks. How I would get around them was a different story. I still had my rifle but was not nearly as skilled as the Troopers who fell the night before. Plus the loud bang would raise alarm and bring who knows how many more to the scene.

I looked around. I still had Elek in my pocket, which was comforting, but even as my "protector" I don't think he could hold off twenty of those beasts alone.

There was a back door to the doctor's office that led into the alleyways that fed into the west side of town. This was my best bet if I was to find the Preacher. Slipping out, I gripped my rifle and went down the alley, through the smoldering remains of building and thick morning air that choked the town.

Hearing a noise, I ducked into a doorway of a half-collapsed building. Footsteps from one of the patrols no doubt. I held my breath as they passed. After the coast was clear I slipped back into the alley and headed for the skeleton of the charred church. Double-checking that it was empty, I entered. Half of the church was completely gone, but if there was any clue that could help me find where the Preacher went, it would be here.

"Hello? It's me, Barnaby," I whispered. My voice sounded flat in what was now the eternal resting place for many who sought shelter during the attack.

"Barnaby?"

"Hello? Preacher? Where are you?" I asked, recognizing his voice.

"Down here." With that the floor in front of the altar lifted, revealing the Preacher, pistol in hand.

"Why do you have a gun?" I wasn't expecting that.

"It's always been the role of the shepherd to keep those in God's flock safe. Sometimes, the tools we need may vary from time to time in order to assure that safety." The Preacher crawled out of the trap door and came over. "Unfortunately, in defending the flock the wolves drew the shepherd away while the others moved in." He looked around to the dead bodies sprawled out on the pews. "I am glad to see that you are well, my friend."

"Yes, I'm fine. But we have to get out of Gideon. Annabelle and Mr. Reynolds are waiting at the doctor's office in the center of town for us. Oh, and Preacher," I paused. "We have to talk." He knew exactly what I meant.

"I knew we would." We wasted no time. After saying goodbye to the Preacher's beloved church we made our way back down the alley. There was no problem getting back to the office, which was odd and sent an uneasy feeling down my spine.

"Annabelle?" I called. entering the room. "Something doesn't feel right." I whispered to the Preacher.

"I know what you mean." He looked around.

"Annabelle." I called again. There was no answer. I ran down the stairs with the Preacher right behind me. The patrol that had passed me in the alley was holding Annabelle and Mr. Reynolds hostage. When they saw us, they took both of them and held them out in front like human shields.

"Drop your weapons," snarled one of the men.

Without thinking I fired a shot. Seeing Annabelle like that sparked something in me, it just came out, something I didn't know I had. It was odd but it made me feel alive. The bullet entered right between the man's eyes; he released Annabelle and dropped to the ground.

The Preacher followed my lead and shot the man that held Mr. Reynolds, then he shot the other two men that had been standing there with swords drawn. Both dropped; the whole thing took mere seconds.

"Annabelle, are you okay?" I asked her.

"I am now." She blushed, causing me to do the same.

"That is the mark of a real trooper, Barnaby." Mr. Reynolds smiled.

"I hate to be the bearer of bad news but those shots were definitely heard. We should move now, Ed," the Preacher turned to him. "All the years I have known your wife she always had a smile on her face. She lived a good life and you were a good husband. May you accept this as peace knowing that she is walking with God now, where she is protected against the intolerance of hate." The Preacher smiled and so did Mr Reynolds. I didn't have the heart to tell the Preacher just yet that God was having his own problems and that this went deeper than we all thought. What was important now was to get everyone safely out of Gideon.

Going back into the alley we began to hear snarls and screams. "What is that?" Annabelle said as she kept pace.

It sounded exactly like the monster Cain turned into. "Don't worry about it—keep moving." We needed to get as far away from that sound as possible.

"There is a stable on the other side of town, where the merchants store their carts," the Preacher pointed out.

"We will take one and go down the road till we find a small wooden cabin. There is a good friend of mine who lives there, he will know what to do." Ed had this all figured out.

We reached the stable while the sounds and snarls grew louder behind us. Everything was set; there was three roads that led out of Gideon, and there were so many tracks leading out of town that our tracks would be blend in.

We all climbed into the cart, except for Ed. "Aren't you coming?" Annabelle asked.

"I have made my decision, I will stay behind. I'll buy you some time." Mr. Reynolds was content with his decision.

"You can't do that!" I tried to convince him. He didn't have to sacrifice himself.

"You don't understand, Barnaby, Gideon is where my entire life rests. I cannot leave now. I have always watched over the people here in one way or another and if I leave now I leave what I love behind."

"Then I'm staying." I said.

"You cannot. I am sorry Barnaby." It was like stepping back in time when Ed was a young trooper, he became the commanding, respectful leader that Darius had looked up to so fondly. Then he hugged me. He looked at me with joy and a deep sense of pride. "I know you will lead the charge another day. Now go." He smiled.

"At least tell me this—why did you retire?" I had to know.

A look in his eyes lifted the age off of his shoulders. "The old must make way for the new. Darius needed to step up and that was the only way."

He did it for Darius, a noble man making a noble decision

for a friend. "I will not forget this." I said climbing into the cart.

"I know you won't." He waved and the horses began to pull the cart at a swift pace. Annabelle and the Preacher sat in the front with eyes ahead. I kept my eyes on the fading Colonel—a brave man who was knowingly and acceptingly waiting for death.

Just as he disappeared from sight, I saw the reptiles surround him, but they did not attack. Another figure emerged from the crowd. I could only make him out because of his blue coat, similar to Mr. Reynolds. Could it be? I thought Darius had said the commander who rode atop the horse died in the marketplace. Then, the man in the blue coat took out a pistol and shot Mr. Reynolds dead. *Why?* Just as I thought I couldn't be any more lost, another mystery presented itself.

— Chapter Seven —

The Parting of Ways

The afternoon came and went as the cart made its way down the trail. All three of us were on the lookout for the small cabin Mr. Reynolds had told us about. There was no one after us at the moment, but still we were pressed for time. It was almost dusk and none of us wanted to be caught outside in the dark.

"Maybe we passed it?" the Preacher questioned.

"It has to be around here somewhere." Annabelle was growing frustrated.

I was still thinking about Mr. Reynolds being killed in cold blood. *Wait till Darius finds out what happened to his beloved mentor,* I thought. *I know he will be crushed.* However, I didn't know if Darius was still alive. The last time I saw him he was being chased by those creatures, and come to think of it, I those creatures are probably demons. If my dreams are what they seem, then I had met God and two of His angels; and if angels existed then surely demons must as well. If demons existed then there was only one conclusion that could be drawn.

God and the Devil, good and evil in their purest form, come together combatively and in the mix of it all is mankind. So if I am right in thinking that both are at war with each other, then why did God present himself to me and why did Cain want me to meet who I can only assume is the Devil?

When I see God again I will have to ask because I can't begin to piece together much more of this. I had lost faith in Him when my family died; now I had to come to terms that He was in fact real. It made me even more angry to know that He existed because He let that happen to them, when He was supposed to love them and keep them safe.

"Found it!" Annabelle pointed victoriously.

We pulled the cart over to the cabin. It was quiet and tiny puffs of white smoke trailed from the chimney. There was an old wooden shed that housed a small pile of hay, this was the perfect place to hide the horses and cart. The Preacher and I readied our weapons.

The door creaked open and we stepped inside. The fire in the fireplace was roaring and the smell of fresh meat and herbs filled the room. "This seems homey," the Preacher lowered his pistol. He was right; between the comfortable looking couches and the soft rug, this place was very luxurious for the Eastern Bounty states.

"Hello." A man, smiling, popped out from the kitchen with two oven mitts on. "Welcome to my home."

"Hello," I said letting down my guard. I had instantly recognized him—it was Angelo.

He looked at me and winked. "Welcome friends, my name is Angelo." He was a lot calmer then last time we met and his wounds were barley visible.

"Hi, my name is Annabelle," she managed to give off a smile but she still held up her guard.

"Hello, I am Josiah Regaul." The Preacher introduced himself.

"I am Barnaby." I said, although he already knew that.

"I hope you found the place just fine." Angelo responded removing one of the mitts and shaking each of our hands.

"Yes, no problem." I answered. "We were sent here by a man named Ed Reynolds. Do you know him?" My curiosity got the best of me. If Angelo had been good friends with Mr. Reynolds, then how far back did this all go? Looking back, I could see that there had been angels intervening in my life before. But maybe this was way more intricate than I imagined. That this all wasn't by chance, it was by design.

Angelo smiled at me like he could read my thoughts. "I have known him for years. How is he?"

The Preacher lowered his head. Angelo took the hint and his tone changed from friendly to disappointed.

"That is indeed a tragedy, he was a man of the greater good. Anyone for bread?" Angelo changed the subject to lighten the mood.

"Thank you." Annabelle responded gratefully.

What did Angelo mean by the greater good? Did Mr. Reynolds know he would have to die? I had to get Angelo alone, I needed to talk with him and figure out my next move. I wasn't sure how I was going to tell Annabelle yet; I knew that telling the

Preacher would be easier considering he is a man of great faith and belief.

Angelo broke bread and we were all given a piece. There was even butter, which I'd had only one other time when I was very young. After eating two very generous slices, I decided that now would be the perfect time to talk.

"Excuse me, Angelo?" I said breaking the silence.

"Yes?" He looked up at me from his plate as if he knew this was coming.

"Can I talk to you for a second?" Annabelle and the Preacher looked from me to him with questioning glances.

"Absolutely," Angelo got up from the table we were sitting at and I followed him into the kitchen. He began kneading dough. "How are you Barnaby?" He lowered his voice.

"I am fine, confused but fine." I answered.

"I figured as much." He chuckled. "It has been a lot to take in I assume. Many questions unanswered and so forth." Angelo pretty much nailed it.

"Exactly. Every time I think that one of my questions is answered another presents itself, it is like a never-ending loop." It was true that I was frustrated and that it bothered me immensely that I couldn't be filled in. I felt like strings were attached to me and I was just being pulled along.

"I am not going to say have faith." Angelo started.

"You aren't?" I cut him off. "But isn't that what you guys are all about, having faith through thick and thin?" This was surprising.

"Why would I say have faith after all you have been through?" Angelo was different from what I thought an angel would be. He could see where I was coming from.

"I am losing it, I don't know what to do. All I wanted was a normal life, I want things to go back to normal, I want a family." I looked up from the kitchen counter at Annabelle.

Angelo smiled. "You love her don't you?" he said, taking me off the subject of this war for a moment.

"Is it too soon to use the word love?" I asked.

"Time isn't a measurement for such words." He advised.

"Good point, but do you think I should even bother? I mean, aren't I supposed to be involved in a war between two forces, who I doubted the existence of no more than twenty-four hours ago?"

Angelo turned this thought over in his head before answering. Then he looked at me with upmost seriousness and passion. "Barnaby, how do you think you are going to win a war without love in your life? Love is the fuel that has driven us this far. What makes you think you are any different from any other man, why are you trying to distance yourself?"

"Because I want her to stay safe, away from the harm that I know will come after me. If I have a chance to deliver her from that evil then I will. To go on with no love is easier than going on with lost love." I couldn't bear the thought; it would tear me apart to see her hurt.

"There is a saying that goes, 'tis better to have loved and lost, than never to have loved at all.' I know you agree, even if you don't want to admit it." Angelo was right. I did agree and I did not want to admit it.

"What if I am not strong enough to lose again?" I asked, I had lost my family, who had meant everything to me. Once Annabelle came into my life I was starting to see a small glimpse of true happiness. Now I was at a crossroads again. I could bring along Annabelle, the Preacher, and every person I meet a long the way, on a path that might get them killed. Or I could choose solitude, where I would face the journey with no fear of risking the lives of those around me. I could get what I needed to get done and there would be no consequence to anyone but myself.

I weighed the options. I had already caused two people to die because I merely came into their lives. Who knew what had happened to Darius, who had taken me under his wing. I was bad luck; death was sure to follow when I was around. All those people in Gideon were dead and they were just bystanders.

"You must not think that way. It is important that you keep those you love close to you. I know it sounds crazy but love must be present." Although Angelo was making a good point, I made up my mind. I was going to leave them all behind during the night. It was the only way to keep them safe, it was the only way in which I would not feel any more pain.

Later that night everyone went to sleep, I was wide awake, fearing another dream, I stayed up sipping tea at the table.

Annabelle was sleeping on the couch and the Preacher was in the other room. Angelo was asleep in a chair.

I guess angels sleep too. It was clear that this would be the best time for me to make my escape. I still had Elek in my pack so I wouldn't be completely alone, but otherwise I was going solo from this point forward. Getting up silently I made my way to the door.

I turned and looked at Annabelle one more time. She was so peaceful and she looked like an angel herself as she slept. I forced my gaze from her and opened the door, stepping outside into the cold dark air. I knew that my path, the destiny that laid ahead, would be equally dark and troublesome. Closing the door I stood outside of the cabin for a brief moment. Second thoughts about running back inside and telling Annabelle I loved her screamed in my head, but they were silenced by the knowledge that soon I would come into danger, and what then? Risk everything by bringing her with me? I couldn't, I wouldn't, I needed to do this on my own, it was safer this way.

"Out for some air?" Angelo was behind me.

"Yeah, just looking at the stars." I said. The stars were particularly bright tonight; the pictures they made in the sky created a shimmering natural show for the world. It was astonishing to think about the distance of that one little speck.

"You know, on cloudy nights when you can only see one or two stars it's nice, but it isn't the same as seeing all of them together, working as one to light up the night." Angelo walked up so as to stand beside me. "For when all of them are working together they make something great." I knew he was trying to get me to stay. I turned to him, stuffing my hands in my pocket and taking a deep breath. But before I could speak, he put his hand on my shoulder.

"Don't. I know this isn't goodbye and I know you are just looking for answers. I understand that when you need to find an answer you don't go asking for one, you have to go looking for one. I like that about you, Barnaby, I have always admired that about you." He smiled. "My only request is that when you do find the answer, remember that you did go looking for it." Then without another word Angelo patted my shoulder and walked back inside.

I knew I had denied help once again from an outside source and that I was being stubborn, but knowing that the Preacher and Annabelle were with Angelo made me feel better.

I wasn't paying much attention to where I was trekking and soon I became lost in the dark woods.

"Well this is great." I grunted. "This is just great."

"Help!" A voice called. It sounded like a woman's voice. "Help!" She sounded weak and afraid.

"Hello?" I called back. I didn't have the heart to leave her out in the woods like this.

"Yes? Hello? Who is that, who are you?" She wasn't very far away, maybe a few dozen yards. But the darkness swallowed everything and anything up causing feet to become miles.

I walked cautiously up to where the noise was coming

from. Curled up on a rock was a girl around my age. She had a black eye and she looked a mess.

"Are you all right?" I was caught off guard by the sight of her. She was very attractive, but by the look of it she was rather beaten.

"Thank you for finding me. I have been out here for hours. These looters came to my home and killed my family. I escaped but barely." She was shaking. She had lost her family like I had; I could relate to the pain she was feeling.

"I am not sure how I can help you." I admitted. I had nothing to give her.

"There is one thing you can do," she said. "My house is a little ways from here. If you could come with me to make sure they are gone then that would be a big help." Something was weird about that idea but she was very distraught and if she lost her family, what was I supposed to say?

"Okay, let's go." We walked down the road, it was eerie but having the company made it easier to keep my cool.

"I am Abigail, by the way." She smiled at me.

"Pleasure to meet you, I'm Barnaby." The conversation was light, she was around my height and she was thin, her long golden brown hair and big smile complemented her eyes. She actually made me miss Annabelle more and more. I wanted to turn around at that moment and find my way back to the cabin to find her. But, a promise is a promise and I would help Abigail find her way back.

"It is just up ahead." She said pointing to a clearing.

We came to a large home, "I don't see anyone," I said looking around. The house looked very nice actually, like it belonged to a nobleman. It had a red roof that curved out in all different directions, with many windows dotting the walls in all shapes and sizes.

"Everything looks good to me, I wish you luck." I went to turn away.

"Wait, what if they are inside? Please, I am all alone." I couldn't leave her. I knew the feeling of being alone after a loss and it was the worst feeling in the world.

We walked inside the dark house and through a parlor that led to a larger room. It was decorated lavishly with ornate art. Comfortable cushioned couches surrounded a fireplace. Standing at the fireplace was a man. At first this gave me a quick jolt. He was wearing a suit, which was very rare and formal around these parts.

"Oh good, you're here." Abigail said in a joyous tone.

"Who is he?" I thought that her family was dead; she didn't mention this man.

The man turned around. He had a glass of some whiskey in his hand and a devilish grin on his face; his eyes glowed like gold in the firelight. In his other hand was a Bible. He carelessly tossed it into the flames as he made his way over to me.

"Oh, you happened to have caught me doing to some light reading. Pardon me, where are my manners, introductions are in order. Hello, Barnaby." He grinned ear to ear.

I turned on the spot but there were two people standing behind me; one of them was the commander from Gideon and the other was a man who looked crude and weaselly. Feeling trapped I ran up the stairs, I had to find a way out.

"Barnaby, you aren't going anywhere. Come back downstairs. Let's have a chat," the man called. The hallway on top of the stairs was lined with mirrors. I had always hated mirrors. I saw the worst of myself when I looked into them; they were my personal hell.

"Hi, Barnaby." Another girl giggled from the hall; she had black eyes and long black hair, with light skin and white teeth. Her boots went all the way up her leg and her torn dress dangled from her body.

I ran in the opposite direction toward a rather large window. Then suddenly, Cain came around the corner. "Remember me?" he grinned as he knocked me out.

I woke up tied to a chair. The six of them stood in a semicircle in front of me.

"You know, you couldn't have made this any easier," Abigail remarked.

"So you don't have a family?" I said spitting blood up from when Cain punched me.

"No, never did. You do though, and I knew you would be obliged to help a poor, helpless girl like myself out who shared your pain." She sounded sweet but her words were stinging.

I tried to break free but all that accomplished was a round of their laughter. I wasn't going anywhere—they knew it and I knew it.

The man who had been standing at the fireplace stepped forward and looked at me like I was a prize. "Welcome. My name is Lennox and I can tell we are going to be very, very good friends."

— Chapter Eight —

The Devil's Den

It all happened so fast. Was I dreaming? Or had I actually fallen into the hands of the very person I was trying to avoid? Time was ticking in the very direction I didn't want it to go. I was so stupid, I should have stayed with the others—why do I always have to be a lone wolf?

My eyes strained to see more than just a blur. I was sitting on a chair, my hands and feet tied down. The room began to fill with detail. I was sitting in an average-sized space, with no furniture to speak of. Except for the elaborate Victorian wallpaper, the room seemed plainer than the other parts of the house. All that covered the floor was a small area rug in a fruit pattern.

I struggled to get my hands free, but after a few tugs I decided it was best to save my strength. "Hello?" I called out. The house was dead silent, like it was built and then instantly abandoned many years ago. It was hard to grasp the feel of this place because it was pleasing to the eye, but at the same time it represented something horrifying. I didn't remember much from last night, it mostly was a collection of images popping in and out, but I did remember the excessive number of mirrors in the hall. Something was off about them that I didn't give much thought to initially. I had never liked mirrors. Was it a coincidence that there were so many here now?

It was clear that Lennox was the Devil, that his merry bunch of Demons were shacked up in this house and orchestrated their plans from within its walls. How I was mixed into this whole situation was still unclear.

The knob on the door shook, then the door creaked open. Two men stepped inside, one of them was the weasel-like man from the night before and the other was the commander from Gideon. "Hello Barnaby," the commander said taking one of the two wooden chairs from the back corner of the room. He placed the chair in front of me while the other man leaned against the wall. "Nice to finally meet you." He smirked and a growing fit of anger boiled up inside me. He had killed Mr. Reynolds in cold blood.

"Why did you kill him?" I barked, I was in no mood for introductions, I hated these people for who and what they were.

"How rude, you shouldn't be raising your voice." He paused. "The name is Vladimir and that is Marx, we have been looking for you for a very long time now. You probably have many questions but I don't really care to answer any of them now. No, no… For now you will tell us what we need to know and then we will discuss other matters." The commander from Gideon, or rather Vladimir, was a Demon all along. He was waiting for me at Gideon, this was unavoidable from the second I got off the train.

"Why did you kill Mr. Reynolds?" I asked again, I wouldn't give them any information until he told me.

"Oh this again," Vladimir got up and walked around my chair, I felt him put his hand on my shoulders. "Barnaby, Barnaby, Barnaby. What are we going to do with you. We ask nicely but you don't seem to want to play nice." As he yanked on the back of my chair and I fell backwards, slamming down hard against the floor. "It is a shame, you know—you could be one of us. It is easier from this side of the fence, especially now. You don't have to pretend to be good all the time. Let loose, be angry." Vladimir taunted me as Marx picked the chair up.

"If you think you are better than us then think again." Marx suggested. "You were born to become one of us."

Through gritted teeth I asked again. "Why did you kill Mr. Reynolds?"

"This little hiccup is getting in the way isn't it?" Vladimir sighed. "All right Barnaby, I'll tell you." He leaned into me and whispered into my ear. "I felt like it."

I wanted to wring his neck. He had killed him for no reason, just to cause me pain. It could have been anyone, anyone who was getting close to me, it didn't matter.

"You tried, now it's our turn " A women's voice called from outside. Vladimir and Marx looked frustrated but they walked over to the door anyway and let two women in. One of them was Abigail, the girl I tried helping the day before, and the other was the witch-like girl I'd encountered in the hallway.

Marx and Vladimir reluctantly left and I was left a lone with them. "You know, he is kind of cute." Abigail said, looking at me and smiling.

"If you like them scrawny," the other laughed. The two encircled me. "Now Barnaby, why don't you help a girl out."

"Last time I did, I ended up tied to a chair." I interrupted. I wasn't buying in to their cute charade.

"Some people like that." Abigail winked at me.

"Come on, we aren't ruthless like the boys. We are caring, nurturing and most of all we will make you comfortable in any way we can. All you need to do is ask. The name is Naomi by the way." She gave off a warm smile but all I could see was the cold soul that was behind the curtain.

"Listen, if you are looking for information then you came to the wrong guy. I don't have anything useful to tell you." I said truthfully.

"Oh but you do, Barnaby." Abigail came closer. She wore tight clothes and high heels. "I'll make you a deal, help us out and we will both help you out." She winked again.

"Get out of my face." I bluntly spat. Abigail came forward now and sat on my lap.

"What are you doing? Get off of me." I tried to wiggle away but I wasn't going anywhere.

"What's the matter, never had a girl sit on your lap before?" She draped her arms around my neck.

"You two would make a lovely couple." Naomi said taking a seat across from us.

"You really think so?" Though Abigail was gleeful I was

dreading the thought.

"Get off of me now," I said sternly; she made my skin crawl.

"Come now, don't make our guest uncomfortable." Lennox entered the room and Abigail jumped off.

"Too late for that." I remarked. Seeing the Devil in the flesh was less frightening than I would imagine. He was a regular man, he didn't have horns or red skin. He wore a tailored suit and the only unique thing about him was his eyes—they were golden with flakes of red swirling around inside. He had a sinister smile that looked as though it could conquer empires.

"Well, from now on things will be different." He turned to the girls. "Leave us." They left the room and we were alone. Lennox took a seat and looked at me like I was some prize pig in the county fair. "I have waited so long for this moment."

"Yeah I know." Having a conversation with Lennox was odd, like nothing I had experienced before, I didn't feel unsafe but at the same time I knew I was in the most dangerous situation I have ever been in.

"Well, you are a rock star in our eyes. Do you know how hard it has been trying to track you down? With those angels, guardians of good or whatever you call them constantly intercepting our plays. It gets rather frustrating when you are trying to set up a new regime, believe me." Lennox must have tried this countless times all throughout my life. I began to question every single person I have ever met.

"Now that you have me what will you do? Kill me?" I asked. Lennox laughed.

"Absolutely not. Why would I kill who is to become my protégé, my greatest work?" Lennox thought of me as a protégé? Why?

"What are you talking about?" I would rather die than become one of them.

Lennox ignored my question and continued. "When I was cast into the deepest and darkest place of God's creation, I made a vow to rise once again and take what is rightfully mine. Well, I have returned, stronger than before, and have taken the first step in claiming the throne." Lennox proudly stated.

"How on Earth does this involve me?" It really didn't make any clear sense.

The Devil snapped. "You are impatient and you complain about being something great, do you know that? You have the power to be a god, but all you can say is 'why me'?" The Devil shook his head. "As I was saying, controlling heaven is not enough to take control of His throne. You must destroy Him." He paused. "Now, I know what you are thinking to yourself. How can this be? Well, I have thought about this for eons and I have found a way in which to do it. Up until now the human race was too preoccupied killing each other with pointless wars. Before that, the human spirit was too strong to influence, but now everything is just right. There is no unity among the people, the classes are too distant. I have grown, and so have you." Lennox smiled. "This is a lot to take in but as I grow, you grow. We are not so different, you and I. You will find as this struggle escalates, you will change in the most fascinating ways." He spoke with great enthusiasm.

"You will find that I will come to disappoint you." I knew I had to die trying to be the good guy because if I didn't, I would watch evil blossom and everything I cared about would perish in its wake.

Lennox was persuasive. "You can hold on to what you hold dear. You don't have to pick and choose like you do when you're a knight in shining armor. Being bad, being good, it's just a perspective and can be easily influenced by words. Do you believe in good? Do you really believe in something that can be tarnished by the natural desire of gain?"

"You are wasting your time." I knew this would upset him and he scowled at me.

"All right, if you don't want to play nice, then I have done all I can do. I will be back tomorrow and the next day, to discuss an end to your feeble teenaged rebellion. Hopefully you will see your true destiny before my patience dries up." The Devil stood, moved the chair back to the corner of the room, and exited.

A mirror formed on the wall directly across from me as the door closed. However, I could not see my reflection—it was like I wasn't there. The frame of the mirror depicted a scene from long ago. Demons and angels fought in the clouds; Michael and the Devil were carved into the crest, swords interlocked. Towards the bottom of the frame demons appeared to be falling into the pit of fire. It was rich in detail and told a tragic story from long ago.

Over the next few hours I sat there, my head was lowered to avoid eye contact with the mirror. I was angry with myself. If I was to become what was expected of me, even if I didn't know entirely what that was, I would have to accept what had happened in my life. I would have to pull myself up by my own bootstraps and press forward, like a man.

The doorknob jiggled once more, startled, I looked up. I wondered, who could it be? To my utmost surprise Michael stepped inside quietly. Was he one of them too? My thoughts went fuzzy like bad static from a television and all I could think about was his massive betrayal of the other angels. He approached me. "Are you all right?"

"What are you doing here?" I whispered trying to kick him. "Are you one of them? How could you do that? I thought even though you were a jerk you were good deep down."

Michael unsheathed his sword and pressed the blade to my neck, "Never again say I am one of them. Do you understand?"

"Yes." I held my breath.

"I am here on my own accord. When we found out about what happened to you, I knew it was up to me to get you out of this mess. You never should have been given the responsibility in the first place to unite us; it cannot be done, especially by you." He began to untie the ropes.

"Why do you hate me?" I simply asked.

"I don't hate you, you and I just have a history," he said as he finished untying my feet, then started on my hands.

"And what would that be?" I had never met Michael before. At least I didn't think so.

"They don't call me Archangel Michael the protector because I like classical poetry, kid. I've seen what you can take, and what they have in store for you is something you won't be able to get up from." Michael was, in his own way, looking out for me. But he did it in a way that made me feel as though I was unworthy of existence.

"Then what do you suggest I do? Roll over and let someone else do the job?" I went back at him as he finished setting me free.

"Precisely. You need not worry about what goes on from this point forward. Barnaby, you aren't going to like what the road ahead of you demands." He was trying to warn me about something.

"You say you know me, and that I should stand aside." I stood up. "That only proves that you don't know me; yes I'm only human, yes I'm unqualified, yes I may seem small in the eyes of an angel. But, I was asked to do something and since everything else has been taken away from me, the only thing I have left is my word and I intend to keep it." We faced off. Michael kept eyeing me, looking for a weakness but at that moment I believe he couldn't find one.

"I can't tell if you're stubborn or stupid." Michael was in deep thought. "Fine, have it your way. I say this again, though. Down this path you will lose everything, you will be torn apart and nothing but an empty shell will be left. I cannot stop you and I will do everything in my power to help you, but I cannot deter the storm that approaches."

I put my hand on Michael's shoulder. "That is all I ask." I smiled at Michael and something changed in the way he looked at me.

"I have to leave now. I will see you again. From here on you conduct this chaos of a concert." Michael went to the door. "But don't expect me to let up. Ropes are only useful when there isn't room for slack." He then opened the door and left, closing it gently behind him. I stood there, processing what had gone on. In a strange way I think I had earned Michael's respect. Or at least I'd shown him that I will take accountability and strive with best effort to face the task ahead.

I had also shown myself that I could become something I never envisioned myself to be—a leader. Sure, I indulged in hero fantasies, but to learn the truth in such a matter was unforeseen. I could feel it, not from just within my dreams as before—but from the outside, from reality, when I was wide awake. It was dancing around me almost as if to say that this is the moment, all aboard.

Dusk turned to night and night to day as I looked out the small stained-glass window. The small scraps of food and little water I was given throughout my stay was just enough to keep me alive. I didn't have an elaborate escape plan; I wasn't tied to the chair anymore but I remained seated because it was either that or the old, creaky wooden floor. I always wondered what hell looked like; I didn't really imagine this though, a nice Victorian home in the middle of the woods. Or maybe this wasn't hell. Maybe this was the Devil's summer cottage. Either way, I had the feeling that if I didn't act fast, I would be trapped here for eternity.

A knock at the door broke the silence on the third day of my captivity. Lennox and the others stepped in all giggling from a prior conversation. "Ah, you are still here." He said looking at the rope that had gathered on the ground. "Barely." Lennox laughed.

"Can I leave now? I think I have proven I am no use to you." I said standing up.

"Now Barnaby. If you were no use to me then I would have disposed of you by now. No, no, I have plans for you, big plans." The others looked at each other and smirked.

"Whatever it is you want, you can forget about it." I spat. I would play no part in their scheme.

"Like you have a choice." Naomi taunted, her lace gloved hands rested on her hips.

"Come now, don't tease the boy, we need him to cooperate." Vladimir glanced at me.

"You are right," Lennox turned to Vladimir then back to me. "How about we have a nice dinner to properly welcome a new member into our growing family. Does that sound good, Barnaby?"

"Do I have a choice?" I asked sarcastically. I knew the answer and the thought of sitting at a table family-style with any of them made me want to throw up.

"No," Lennox affirmed. "Although, if you behave I'll let you sit next to Abigail," he winked at me and Abigail gave me a seductive look from the doorway. Don't get me wrong, I hated the lot of them, but there was something particularly vile about her.

Lennox gestured to the door. "Come, Barnaby. It is time to dine with the Devil."

— Chapter Nine —

Dining with the Devil

The table was long and covered in a spotless white cloth. Illuminated by dozens of candles, the spread drew from every culture, from all walks of life. I will admit I was impressed and surprised. The cushioned seats of the ornate antique chairs seemed out of place. I mean I didn't expect to find comfort in the same room as the Antichrist. Classical music started to play out of nowhere. Lennox was not only well-versed in cultural indulgences, but found ways to make his unpleasant presence bearable. At that moment I learned the Devil's greatest attribute—persuasion. This gave me an idea.

If I was to start a resistance in order to combat Lennox and his demonic army, I would have to know him better than his top advisors. I had to become his absolute right-hand man; I had to become his friend. As I rolled this thought over in my mind, I instantly saw repercussions and needed to address those before I made my first move. From a very young age I was always given the advice to measure twice, cut once.

Annabelle popped into my head. Becoming an ally with Lennox would mean permanently cutting ties with her, not that there were many to begin with. However, if I did befriend him I would increase the odds of not only saving her but ensuring her future. And that was my goal; though God asked me to do this, I still had my own reasons for going through with it.

I didn't waste time getting my newly formed plan into action. Filling my plate with the fare around me I began to eat. This surprised them because it was the first time I looked remotely close to enjoying myself in their company. I had to be careful in my next step; it wasn't enough for me to give in to their request to join them at the table. I would need to interact with them as well. That was step two: try and lure them into a false sense of security. Lennox wants me to be his prized pig? Then I'll make sure that he gets his blue ribbon.

"So Lennox, nice taste." I said as I took a forkful of the first thing I could get hold of.

He looked at me and for a moment I thought my plan was going to spoil, but then he took a large slab of meat and put it on his plate, cut a piece and popped it into his mouth. He lifted his fork again and pointed to various fixtures and carvings. "These are inspired from royal families throughout history. I find history to be fascinating, especially its architecture. The style of architecture and the materials they use to create their monuments and dwellings tell you just as much about a culture as its food." He laughed and I laughed along. "Wine?" He asked. I nodded and my glass instantly filled. I took it and swirled it in my hand then took a sip. I had to keep calm; so far, so good.

"What do you like most about architecture?" I asked trying to sound engaged.

"Good question." The Devil was loving the attention. "I

find the amount of resources and hours spent in erecting these religious monuments to be not only intriguing but also comedic."

"How so?" I quickly asked as if I was on the edge of my seat.

"For starters, I have never seen anything questioned as much as religion, but then people spend so much time putting it up on a pedestal, clinging to it like it will save them. Seems like a double-edged sword to me, they will say **sure I believe,** but they only say that because they have nothing to lose if nothing is there. But if something is there, then everything is to be gained."

"The question was not your stance on religion." I joked knowing that if I get Lennox into some sort of debate, I will be seen as more of an asset because I can evoke thought and not just take up space.

"You asked me what I like most about architecture, the social belief system is a part of our fabric, and what we are made of is certainly classified under the definition of architecture." The Devil's way of speaking was nothing I have ever heard before. He choreographed his words like the finest ballet.

"I never thought about it that way." I admitted.

"What are your thoughts? What is your favorite aspect of man's insight to this world and the next?" The Devil took another piece of red meat and popped it into his mouth.

"Well…" I needed to step up the conversation to keep the Devil's interest. Even though he needed me around he didn't need to tell me anything about him that I could potentially use in the future to my advantage. "I see it as this. Man has created a material belief that has taken us from the path that faith once was. We must make ourselves comfortable with the notion that our eyes will close one day and our mouths will shut. I genuinely believe that there is good and that people do believe in some higher power. That said, I do see your point: the double edge of the blade shines brighter on the side of the ones who turn to religion for convenience." He looked at me and then to the others.

"You see, this is the purest example of good dinner conversation. It is not only a feast for our physical appetites but the appetite that stimulates our thoughts." Marx and Naomi looked at each other and rolled their eyes. The Devil in the most gleeful manner picked up a dinner roll and ripped it open. "Barnaby, so you are telling me that through material things, these cowards can hide behind religious symbols and titles in order to guarantee a spot on the other side of the street? That their questioning will go unnoticed because as you said, those who say they believe do so, so that they don't find themselves on the receiving end of that sword?" I had the Devil right where I wanted him.

"Precisely." I said raising my glass.

After dinner I was led back upstairs to the room. However, it wasn't the same room I left; now it was lavishly furnished. Lennox must have ordered it during dinner. The carvings on the frame of the bed held the most comfortable mattress; I still couldn't see myself in the mirror, but it didn't bother me as much, for tonight I won a small victory. My plan was working and though I was still in the clutches of the Devil, I took comfort in knowing that something was acting in my favor. I had convinced Lennox that I shared similar beliefs; this only added to his belief that he and I were alike. I had fooled him into thinking that a majority of faith is nothing more then a charade, when in fact it is the farthest thing from.

I was allowed to sleep in, the smell from the kitchen downstairs seemed designed for my taste buds. Getting dressed I walked downstairs and saw that a creature was hunched over a large pot. It turned around and looked at me. It looked like a fish and though it seemed harmless when it smiled and bowed its head to me, I noticed rows of razor sharp teeth.

"Ah, I see you have met my butler." Lennox came over to me, he was finely dressed, holding a glass of brandy. "Are you wondering what it is?"

"Yeah," I said still slightly taken back by the creature.

"His name was William Wayne, a famous fisherman of his time. He used to take women with him on his ship, mostly prostitutes, when he set sail in the morning. By nightfall his ship would be filled with hundreds of fish. This went on for years. All the other fishermen would beg to be his deckhand because he was becoming wealthy from his reputation at the market.

If you are wondering what happened to the prostitutes, it isn't hard to figure out. Apparently they made good bait.

One day a young poor boy snuck onto his ship, and when

the ship returned that night the boy reported what he had seen to the police. Mr. Wayne went out the next day on schedule and was met by the U.S. fleet. They searched his ship, then used him and his beloved boat for target practice. He sank to the bottom of the bay, until I made him a deal." The Devil looked at him with disgust.

"What was the deal?" The story was disturbing. I couldn't imagine what those poor women went through.

"In return for not spending an eternity in hell, he shall be my servant and never, ever go near the water again." He said in a distant voice. "For even more than killing, he loved the touch and smell of the water."

"Why does he look like that?" I asked. He was fish-like with whiskers, large eyes, and an equally large head. His feet didn't look like they were suitable for walking or swimming and the fin along his back disappeared into a goldfish-like tail.

"I don't actually know, I did let his body rot amongst the fish for three hundred years, or it could his tremendous guilt that unleashed his inner animal, a slimy little creature from the sea. But, who cares? What he did was worthy of the outcome." The Devil seemed to disapprove of William's villainy.

"No offense, but shouldn't you applaud him? I mean you are the Devil, aren't you?" Lennox looked at me and walked into the next room.

"Come Barnaby," he called. I walked into the parlor and saw that he was sitting on a lush couch of violet and red. "Take a seat." He gestured to the identical couch adjacent to him. "Would you like some?" He gently shook his glass of brandy as I took a seat.

"No thank you." I said.

"All right, what was your question again?" he asked.

"I was wondering why you were upset with William, why you aren't impressed with what he did." There was silence and for a second I thought Lennox was going to dismiss my question and lock me up again, but in his eyes was just an essence of calm serenity.

He began. "Well Barnaby, my position in the ranks of time is to be the keeper of those who do wrong during the mortal years. Either for just a short time, or until they have a chance to redeem themselves by being thrown back into the bowl of life. Do I agree with what they do? Absolutely not. I am a figure, not a monster."

"Then why do you persuade people to make the wrong choice?" I asked the Devil, I had seemed to peel back a layer of Lennox that was unknown, maybe even to him.

"I encourage an evil act so that the cat and mouse may chase themselves," he said taking another sip.

"What?" I didn't get what he was trying to say.

"I am the cat, chasing the poor mice who are just trying to live their lives. Sometimes I catch the mouse and it is indeed a tragedy, but other times I won't, and it is indeed triumph. Don't you see? You cannot have a sunny day without some rain, the gloomy day of rain will also water the ground, making the trees grow tall and the people may sit under their shade." Lennox set his glass onto a table.

"You only do what you do because you know good will follow?" I asked. This was crazy; the Devil fancied himself as the man who kept the circle spinning.

"Maybe, but you have to admit—it gets kind of lonely around here, especially when everyone is rooting for the other guy. I'm just trying to make some friends." The Devil shrugged.

— Chapter Ten —

Resurrection

The next six months were a whirlwind of information. Almost every night the Devil and I would retire to the parlor where we would discuss matters of human nature and history. Every subject was covered and it came to the point where I didn't see the others as much around the house. I wouldn't say we were pals, but I found that my plan was becoming less and less of a focus.

"How is the crusade?" I asked, sipping the brandy that I had now become accustomed to accepting.

"I find no need of it now. I have captured Heaven and the globe, and I already have Hell to call my own—what else do I need? The throne of God?" He laughed, taking another sip. "You know what? Let Him keep it, if He and the rebels want to keep fighting let them. I don't care." The Devil didn't see them as a problem; he didn't care that God was still out there.

"Aren't you afraid?" I asked.

"Afraid of what?" Lennox poured more brandy. "Do you know how weak He has become? You can more than measure his strength unlike the days of yesteryear." He took a rather large sip and looked at me like a father would look to his son. "Barnaby, do you know what we can accomplish together?"

"Anything?" I said as I poured myself another glass.

He stood up, wobbled and then found his footing.

"Precisely, it is our time. I know you have been dealt a terrible hand in the past, you have been knocked down and left to die. But, I will lift you up and we shall stand side by side as equals. Which hemisphere do you want to reign over? Either one, I don't care." The Devil was tipsy, I didn't think that was possible but he was high on victory so I guess that pushed him over the edge.

I laughed. "I think you've had enough." I said standing to take his glass.

He sat back down. "You always know what's best for me."

I sat again and put both glasses onto the table. "So, what now?" I asked. "Does this mean peace?"

"Peace? Ha, I know nothing of the word. Peace is reserved for those who are tired, but I am inspired."

"I thought you said you didn't care?" I said, hoping the Devil would leave the rebellion alone. I knew Annabelle was still out there, fighting.

"I won't be the first to attack, does that please you?" Lennox asked.

"Yes." I simply said, I was content with that answer.

There was a scuffle from the next room as the door swung open. We saw that Vladimir, Marx, Abigail and Naomi were all holding someone—a man with dark skin and chocolate eyes. He looked weak from exhaustion but was built like a foundation. He wore tattered clothes and at his side rested a horn. He looked up at me and gave a look of disappointment and sorrow. My stomach turned; he knew who I was and I knew who he was. He was an angel. There was no question of what would happen to him here.

"Ah, Daniel. Nice of you to join us." The Devil smirked.

"Believe me, the pleasure is all mine." Daniel said sarcastically.

"Charming." Lennox continued. "To what do I owe the honor?"

"Cut the hospitality, it doesn't suit you. Kill me now and be done with it." Daniel knew he was going to die.

I wanted to help. I didn't want to see anyone die, but what was I going to do? Face four demons and Lennox by myself? But if I didn't, then I would be sitting back while they murdered an angel, the side I'm supposed to be on.

"All right, since you are in such a rush to die I guess I'll grant your wish. Any last words?" Lennox crossed his arms, bored.

Daniel shook the four Demons away and knelt before us. He looked at me. "When the cavern we are trapped in becomes darkest, light will appear once more, and a rope will bear down upon us and pull us to safety."

I turned to Lennox. He nodded at Vladimir and before I could stop him, I saw Vladimir's blade go through Daniel like he was nothing but paper. Daniel fell to the ground and silence filled the room.

"Where did you find him?" Lennox asked.

"Wandering around the grounds." Marx was proud of his

discovery.

"There could be more, we should act now." Naomi wanted a fight; all of them did. While Lennox and I were yukking it up, the others had been bottled up in the house like caged dogs.

"Doesn't seem to be a threat to us now, why stop the party?" I was shocked. Lennox did not feel the need to go out, find more angels and kill them like the others. Could I have changed the Devil's mind about this whole conflict? If so what would become of the world? It was still controlled by the demonic armies under Lennox's command. However, they wanted to cleanse the world of the remaining angels and even God Himself, while Lennox thought of them as just merely existing and not contributing to anything worth noting.

"We can't just sit here," Vladimir raised his voice.

"He is right, we want war." Naomi added.

"And the blood of those who cast us to die." Marx spat on Daniel's still body.

"I don't mind. I'm a lover, not a fighter." Abigail winked at me; after all this time she still bothered me most of all.

The fire in the fireplace erupted and they lowered their heads to avoid his gaze. "We will do things my way and my way only, understood?" Lennox spoke calmly but with intimidation.

"Sorry." Vladimir said through clenched teeth.

"If it means that much to you though, since I am in a good mood, I will listen to your concerns. Come." Lennox walked into the next room and the others followed. I was left standing there all alone, except for the body of Daniel a few feet from me.

When the coast was clear and I was sure I would have a minute to myself I walked cautiously to him. I knelt down and put my hand on the wound. I didn't mind that blood seeped onto my hand. His blood would forever be on my hands anyway, I had done nothing to stop this. "I am sorry," I said beginning to shake.

"Did you understand?" He whispered. I jumped back. He was still alive? I composed myself.

"Understood what?" I asked trying to keep my voice down.

"You needed to be shown that we were still out there, waiting for you." He smiled and more blood seeped onto the floor.

"Are there many more of you? Who is left? Is Annabelle with you?" I asked feverishly.

Daniel just smiled. "Take the horn, you are now the judgment." He grabbed my arm and a blue water like veil engulfed us then dissipated. He looked up to the ceiling, smiled, and closed his eyes. I sat for a few moments, said a small prayer and gripped the horn tightly. It was his last gift and I was the recipient.

"You all right?" A voice came from the doorway. I looked up, it was Cain. I had always been more leery about him than I was the others, he came and went more often and Lennox didn't have much of a say in what he did since Cain acted first and then asked permission. In the six months I was there I almost had a scuffle with Cain a few times; he didn't like me and I could pretty much say the same about him. He led the charge that killed so many in Gideon and who knows what else.

"Oh, yeah I am fine, I was just making sure he wasn't breathing." I said trying to cover my tracks.

"Mind helping me dispose of this filth, it's getting on the carpet," he said, smirking. He sickened me but anything he might have seen could get me killed by the others. I would have to play along.

"Wouldn't mind at all." I grabbed Daniel's ankles and Cain grabbed his shoulders. We walked outside and into the front yard.

"Right here should be fine, he can be a testament to what dwells inside," Cain laughed and set the fallen angel's body onto the ground. I did the same and after he retrieved two shovels we began to dig. It was a shallow grave but it was more of a proper burial than I thought Cain was going to give him. The moment was sweet for Cain and full of sorrow that I tried not to show.

Cain finally spoke breaking the silence. Leaning on his shovel he squinted at me, trying to decode my thoughts. "You're weak."

"Excuse me?" I wasn't surprised by this statement. Plenty of people had called me weak.

"But, you are up to something and I can't tell if you are going about it in some ingenious way or are just really stupid." Cain was sensing my paranoia; this was the first time here that my motives had been questioned.

"What do you mean?" I asked, trying to play dumb; it was

the only defense I could think of.

"Don't act like you don't know, you are acting like a puppeteer, and just know that one day you will be caught, tangled in the same strings."

I slammed the door to my room. I was being found out by Cain. It would be only a matter of time until the others knew that I had been playing them for my own personal gain.

My eyes had been opened by the death of Daniel the angel to judgment day. How could I have let this go on for this long? How could I have sat back and let the Devil become, dare I say, a friend? I wanted to scream, I wanted to bang my head against the wall till I was nothing but mush.

"What are you so upset about?" A familiar voice filed the room. No one but me was there and I looked around.

"Who was that?" I snapped.

"It's you," the voice answered.

"What?" I didn't know what was going on, my head felt like a weight was just dropped onto it. I had no time for games.

"Over here in the mirror." The voice was coming from the side of the room where the mirror hung.

I walked over and as always I did not see my reflection. Someone was playing a prank on me. "What is happing to me?" I shook my head and turned away.

"Look closer." It was indeed my voice, I looked back once again and this time the mirror was different. My reflection was looking right back at me, but it wasn't a mirrored image it was like another Barnaby.

"Hello?" I said, cautious and confused.

"Well, hello there. I've been waiting for the chance to talk to you." My reflection smiled back at me; while I was on the verge of freaking out, he was as calm as a spring breeze.

"You wanted to talk to me? About what?" I understood at this point that anything was possible but there are some things that a person could never get used to, and a talking mirror was one of them.

"About you, about me, well about us technically," he said.

"What about us? Is this even happening right now?" No sane person has a conversation with themselves and actually gets an answer.

"Fortunately for me, yes, it is happening right now." My other self was pretty excited to get a chance to talk to me. I didn't share the same feeling, though.

"What do you want?" I asked, pushing for some answers.

"I am here because there is something you need to know."

"Aren't we the same person, don't we share the same knowledge, everything you know I probably already figured out, right?" It was the only logical thing I could think of, I mean, how much could he have known that I didn't?

"You see things from the outside, from the present as they are happening. I see things from the past, the present and the future because I am from within and therefore without need to react. I have perspective while you have your best guess." All right,

133

maybe my inner self knew more than I give him credit for, but I was still hesitant.

"Well put, go on." I said.

"To make things simple, just listen and don't ask questions." He continued. "We are the same in a sense but different by birth. We exist together but cannot be farther apart." He stopped and laughed. "I know this sounds like some weird poetic description of two people living as one person but believe me, that is the only way to describe what we have here." My other half went on. "We both have a job to do. Yours is by request and mine is by nature." He cleared his throat. "Let me introduce myself, I am your greatest asset and the last nail that will be driven into your coffin." A pause left me on the edge of my seat. "Troubling times are ahead for you, and since I am attached to your hip I guess I am in for the same ride. But it comes down to this: you need to get yourself in gear, look at yourself and ask. **What is a man measured by?**

"What do you mean?" Truthfully I had no idea.

Myself turned around in the mirror and walked to the nightstand. He pulled out a small stone statue, and held it out in front of me, this turned my perspective around. "This is Elek, the protector. What happened to him?"

I looked down shamefully, "I shut him away."

"Need I say more?" he said calmly, his point proven. "You had good intentions in giving your word that you will undermine this chaos, but thus far you have only supplied its tinder."

I looked up with the same sorrow I'd felt watching Daniel die. "What will you have us do?"

Smiling, my reflection said one word.

"Resurrect."

— Chapter Eleven —

Evil's Broken Heart

There was a knock at the door, but I remained in bed facing the painted ceiling. A while back I had requested the "Creation of Adam" that was painted by Michelangelo on the Sistine Chapel's ceiling as a joke. Lennox had the most accomplished painters in history make it happen. Anything I wanted was just a command away. I was disgusted by what I had become. I had a sinking feeling that I had dropped the ball and that it was too late. Another knock at the door stirred me, and before I could get up to answer Abigail entered.

"Hello." She was bubbly, wearing a short dress. When you think "demon" you definitely don't picture something like that. However, surrounding her was a feeling of unease.

"Hi." I blankly answered. I never gave her the time of day. I felt it was best.

"You feeling all right?" she asked, coming closer to the bed.

"Yes, I'm fine." My blank response held its own against her flirtatious pose. I still had Annabelle on my mind constantly— wondering if I would ever see her again and wondering if she even wanted to see me again. I had left her and the Preacher without even a goodbye; it seemed harsh after what we had gone through together.

A look of frustration washed over Abigail. "I am fine, thanks for asking." I knew that she was trying to pull a conversation out of me; this had been routine for the past four months. Usually I locked my door, but I must have forgotten under the circumstances earlier today.

"I have to wash up, dinner is soon." I said sitting up. It wasn't a good idea to be horizontal in the presence of Abigail, I had learned this from experience regrettably. Luckily, Lennox was there to put a stop to it.

"You know, you're going to be here for a very long time; you may as well just give in to it." She jumped onto the bed.

"It isn't going to happen. I'll see you at dinner." I said getting up and walking to the door.

"No you won't, I already ate. So, when you have had your fill you can come back upstairs and have your fill of me." She winked and my skin crawled. "I'll be waiting."

"Terrific." I moaned as I went into the hallway. Mirrors lined the walls but I kept my eyes forward. I didn't want to run into myself again and feel worse than I already did. I didn't know how to escape, but I needed to figure it out tonight.

I walked into the dining room. Marx and Vladimir were already having a debate about drawing out the rebel angels. They looked at me and smiled.

"Ah, Barnaby, you are here." Vladimir said. In recent weeks I had won over their friendship as well, though I didn't really want or need it.

"I can hear you arguing over Abigail's attempts to seduce me." I said making them erupt into laughter. Everyone knew that Abigail had an unhealthy desire for me, so whenever she got a little touchy, either Marx or Vladimir would make a joke so she would run off. That was one thing I did appreciate.

"Hey listen, Barnaby can you settle an argument for us?" Marx said as he ate a hearty steak.

"Sure, what's up?" I said as I sat down, picking up my fork and knife.

"How do you think we should combat these rebels?" Marx's question bothered me. For months they hadn't paid much attention to the cause of the rebels and surviving angels, but since Daniel's appearance, they wanted to kill them all in one great swoop.

"Marx thinks we should send in an informant, someone who will gain their trust, then strike while their backs are turned. I say that they are too smart for that and that we need a direct military approach to blow them away with sheer volume. Any thoughts?"

I took my time before answering. I made the two of them watch me for a few moments in anticipation for my answer. I worried more about how good the food tasted than the actual question, to be honest. I didn't want to discuss matters of killing the people I would be seeking out to help me in my quest— especially with the people who I intended to kill in the process. "Well," I began as I wiped my mouth with my napkin, "why do we have to leave our comfort zone to go looking for them? Why don't we just let them come to us? Daniel did and look where we are now because of it."

Vladimir and Marx looked at each other and smiled. "I like this guy." Marx said, grinning like a barfly.

"Nice of you to join us." Vladimir was looking at the doorway where Lennox stood. Lennox looked serious and not like his more recently happy self.

"Leave." He gestured toward Marx and Vladimir. The two left without a word and the Devil sat right next to me; usually he would take a seat at the other head of the table.

"Everything all right?" I asked, holding my breath. Cain must have told him that I was not who I claimed to be. If Lennox had found out the truth, then surely this would be my last night alive.

"I was thinking about the death of Daniel today, and something hit me." Lennox seemed upset; did he know I took the horn? Was he upset that I had lied to him about the friendship we had forged?

"What?" I asked sliding my plate away.

"I have to be more sensitive towards you. I mean no less than a year ago you were on the side of God. I can't expect you to accept the way we act and the way we deal with our enemies, it isn't in your nature to kill, Barnaby, I know this."

I was stunned by what Lennox had said, he was trying to be sensitive? It was like he changed over the course of my stay. He seemed to take me under his wing and protect me from things in life such as death. I knew at that moment I would have to make the most dangerous call of my entire life—leave the Devil now or forever stay at his side. The only thing was, I didn't know how he would react to my betrayal.

The conversation for the rest of the meal was light. It was just the two of us and for me it was a blur. I still couldn't imagine the Devil becoming soft towards anything; was this better or was this in no uncertain terms worse, way worse?

I closed the door behind me and in a rush I collected my few belongings.

"Hey there." Abigail was indeed waiting for me on the bed. She had hiked her dress up to the point where imagination was just inches away from becoming obsolete.

"I don't have time for you right now." I said to her as I pushed her to the other side of the bed. I opened the nightstand and saw what I had ignored, my true purpose. Inside that tiny knitted pouch was Elek. He was my true protector, not Lennox.

"What you got there?" I felt Abigail's soft hand hold me from behind as she looked over my shoulder.

"None of your business." I said knocking her off. I slipped him into my pack and was ready. Even in the dark I would pray for light to be my guide as I ran as fast as I can away from this house of hate.

"Going somewhere?" Cain was standing in the doorway. He looked at me in hatred and glee. He had waited for this moment—for how long, I don't know.

"No," I said, remaining calm.

"Why would he be going anywhere?" Abigail said walking to my side and taking my hand. I let her hold my hand so it would convince Cain otherwise. She seemed to be surprised that I let her do this and she instantly took advantage of the situation. "We were kind of in the middle of something," she said, going to the door. She tried to close it, but he stopped her.

"He is lying," Cain kept his gaze on me.

"Let go of me," she demanded.

"She isn't apart of this. It's just you and me. Leave her out of it." Even though Abigail gave me the creeps, she still was a person, more or less.

"All right," Cain smiled and pushed Abigail against the wall. He came at me but I was ready for this moment. Out of everyone in the house I wanted to take him out the most. Ever since our encounter in Gideon I personally linked him to the deaths of those poor people and now was my chance to show them that they were remembered.

We stumbled onto the bed and punches flew like a flock of birds, fast and in every direction. Abigail tried to pry Cain off of me but he pushed her away once more. Managing to get distance from Cain, I jetted down the hallway and stairs. He was hot on my tail; if I could get outside, maybe I could outrun him. The odds were slim, but they were better than staying here fist to fist with a demon.

I had my hand on the knob of the front door when he pulled me back and into the parlor. He threw me onto the sofa and laughed. "I knew it, you think you can defeat me! I killed my own brother. What makes you think I won't kill you?"

I was aching but I stood up. "Because I have my word to keep."

Growling, he lunged for me, although this time I was charged with purpose and promise. Catching him, I used his momentum to pick him up and slam him down on the table where the Devil and I had had countless conversations. Not wasting time, I ran for the door. The fresh crisp night air felt good against my burning cheeks. I felt like I was free. I was free.

"Barnaby!" Lennox's voice called from the door. I stopped in mid-sprint and turned. Lennox, Vladimir, Naomi, Abigail, Marx and a sore Cain stood on the porch. "Where are you going?" He and the others looked confused, Abigail looked as if she was on the verge of tears and Cain scowled at me.

"I have to leave. This isn't my place, this isn't me." I knew there was no turning back now.

"I considered you a son!" he yelled.

"I know, and I am sorry." I took a few steps backwards.

"Cain." Lennox said as he started to growl himself.

"Yes?" Cain approached him as if reporting for orders.

"Did you harm him in any way?" Lennox was getting hysterical and his voice was shaky.

"He was trying to escape." Cain reported. But as he did a

sword was thrust into his chest. He fell to his knees, the Devil then lopped his head clean off.

The others stood there in silence and Abigail's faint crying could be heard. "See Barnaby? I can make your life better. Cain was your enemy; look what I can do to your enemies! This is all for you. Please stay." Lennox begged.

"I am sorry, but from now on, you are my enemy." I was surprised that there was no pleasure in my voice. It wasn't that I wanted to be friends with the Devil, but he looked so sad it was natural to feel pity.

Everything was still. "Then if I can't have you, no one can." In fury Lennox turned to his remaining core of demons. "Hunt down and slit the throats of every angel and every God damned rebel. The war is back in full throttle. May the days of mercy be but history." He looked back at me. "And for you. I will personally save you for last, after every single one you know is hunted down and viciously torn apart. Their deaths will be on your hands and their faces will haunt your dreams for the rest of days." I had awoken an evil far greater than the one before. I had taken something from the Devil that meant more to him then the lonely throne of power.

I expected a chase; I expected to run for my life. However, the Devil just turned and went back into the house. The others looked at me then followed their wounded leader. Was that it? I counted to five in my head. I didn't want to turn my back just yet; I wanted to make sure the coast was clear.

A few hours later, reality hit me as I walked away from the house. I had made things worse, but for the better. Turning away from the Devil's side did reignite this conflict into a full blaze, but it also showed me that my path of saving the good was now more important than ever. Although it killed me to say it, I knew I couldn't do it alone. I would need once again to use Neo's advice and make friends.

Reaching into my pack, I took out Elek and unwrapped him. I had completely forgotten about him, I forgot about everything that was asked of me. Well, not anymore. "I promise to do better." I said clutching him.

Without warning he shook. I dropped him and stepped back. Before my eyes he morphed from pocket size to larger than life. He looked down at me. Tiny pieces of stone had been chipped away during his fight with Cain in order to protect me. He would protect me at all costs, and I had taken him for granted.

"I want to say, I'm sorry." I said sincerely.

Elek went to kneel before me, but I couldn't let him do that—who was I?

"No, stay." I said having an idea. I knelt in front of him and bowed. He was the one who deserved it. "I can't do this without you. You are my protector after all."

I felt myself being picked up. Elek looked at me and smiled, showing his stone fangs. "No. I am Elek, a friend." I smiled, knowing that though things would be tough from here on, I would still get through it all.

He set me on my feet and I felt that everything was in line, except for one thing; I had no idea what our next move was going to be. "Listen Elek, I am sorry. I don't exactly know what I am doing."

Elek looked at me. Though he had a more lifelike quality, he was still very much a statue. "I have an idea." He turned around and spread his wings. "Get on." I hesitated, then climbed onto his back.

"Where are we-" Before I could even get out the rest of my sentence, he jetted off into the night air. Wind whipped my face and my stomach felt the same as it did the night I first saw Annabelle. I couldn't help but laugh. Surprisingly, it was easy to hold onto him and I found myself feeling safe. *Can you believe this?* I asked myself. *Can you believe everything that has happened, both good and bad?*

I found myself looking back into the bakery window on that cold night. The man named Edmund had given me not only bread, but hope. I didn't know if he was one of the angels who had come into my life to guide me onto the right path, but he was an angel in my book for sure for what he had done—with or without wings.

— Chapter Twelve —

The Heap

"Welcome back," Michael said from across the table.

"W-what?" I groaned, sitting up, drool running down to my chin.

"How was your trip?" Fay asked, smiling at me.

"Wait—I'm supposed to be with Elek, not sitting here." My head was pounding.

"You are with him, but you fell asleep on his back. That is why you are here." Michael looked at me, displeased, and I knew why.

There were other angels in the room, each with a varying expression of rejoicing.

"Since most of us haven't met Barnaby before, let's introduce ourselves as one now. We have a lot to talk about," Fay suggested.

A man began to speak. I recognized him instantly; it was Jason. "Hello, Barnaby. I am Raphael, the angel of both guidance and healing; you can call me Jason."

The next person spoke immediately after. "I am Hayyel, the angel of wildlife. You will call me Ariel." Ariel had wavy red hair and an accent that I heard once before, but only when an Irish pastor came to visit our church many years ago. She had green eyes. But more striking was the green and gold tattoo of a vine with bright leaves on the side of her neck. She was also thin and her nose came to a point that titled slightly upwards.

"You already know me," Angelo smiled, "but I am Gabriel—a messenger by trade, of course."

Next was Fay, but she just waved at me.

The next angel was different from the others. He was of Asian descent, very old, with a receding hairline and long beard. He looked at me through thin glasses and smiled. "Hello, I am Bath Kol, I hold the prophecy of every encounter. Please call me Ramelan." He smiled again; this time I noticed he was missing some teeth.

Next was a very young girl. She had wavy cream colored hair and bright blue eyes. She was adorable in her little blue dress, the definition of innocence. "Hi mister," she said with a bright smile and wave. "I am Israfel, but you can call me Carol. I love to sing."

She was sweet. They all were nice. I can't believe I turned my back on them. To think, if things had been different, Daniel could be standing here as well. I sank in my chair trying to hide myself in shame.

"What is wrong?" Fay asked in a motherly tone.

"What isn't wrong?" Michael said. "We are behind schedule and while you were playing patty cake with Lennox we have been getting it handed to us on every front."

Michael was clearly angry, and I could tell everyone else

agreed with him.

"I will not have you blame him. In fact, I expect you to congratulate him." God's voice once again filled the room. The other angels standing around the table cleared way for God to step forward. "Welcome back, Barnaby. How have you been?"

"I am so sorry." I blurted out. He smiled and the others didn't seem to find the apology necessary either.

"Don't waste your words, Barnaby, it was actually beneficial. You now know the workings of your enemy." God was right, my original plan had been to find out more of who the Devil actually was. I had done that, I had all the information I possibly needed. I had more fire power than any weapon I could get my hands on.

"I have a question." I asked looking around at everyone. It wasn't important, and it wasn't the topic of current discussion, but it did just occur to me. "Why don't you use your angel names? Why use other names?" Michael chuckled like he thought my question was stupid. "Because he can walk freely around if everyone thinks his name is Jason." He gestured to Jason. "No demon is going to say, hey look, there is Jason the angel of healing. They will be suspicious if a man is going around with a name like Raphael." Michael had a point and everyone nodded to his answer.

"Than why don't you have a name?" I asked Michael.

Although Michael was a common name, I am sure they didn't want to leave anything up to chance.

"Because, unlike the rest of this lot, I am not afraid of the consequences that might come with being found." Michael was always playing the macho card.

"We are not afraid, but if we hope to stop the dark we must ensure we are able to fight another day." Ramelan pointed out. "You will never win a war if you do not blend into your surroundings, adaptation is key."

"We'll see old man." Michael yet again was drawing tension into the room.

"Enough Michael, this is not the time to argue." God released the tension and everyone was calm once more.

After a moments pause, everyone drew their attention back to me. "So what is our next step?" I asked trying to break the silence.

"That is up to you." God answered. "You see, we are all scattered around the world. None of us are actually here right now. For you to find us, you must assemble a team to help you, each with a different strength, for it is not the job of one type of person. When the time comes, you will know where to look."

This was unexpected. I would have to get together a bunch of people and in order to do that I needed to convince them to go on a wild goose chase all around the world, without any direction, to find angels who are in hiding—not only once but possibly dozens of times.

"How am I supposed to do that? If I didn't have a plan before, I definitely didn't have one now."

"You can do it, I have faith in you." Fay smiled and so did Carol.

"You already know where one of us can be found." The voice of Edmund spoke up. "I believe we met once before." He came through the crowd and stood beside God. I smiled.

"I knew you were an angel!" I let out. Everyone laughed except Michael, who just crossed his arms.

"Yes, I am, and I think that you should stop by my shop again. This time you don't have to stand in the window." He smiled and I back at him. He had saved my life, as far as I was concerned I owed everything to him.

"What are you the angel of?" I asked him.

"He is the angel of the guardian, and I, of liberation." A bald man with white piercing eyes stepped out from the crowd. He was the thief from the church.

"Relax, I was only doing what was asked of me. My name is Baron, by the way." He nodded.

"I don't care what your name is, you tried to kill me in the barn and then you hit me on the head and knocked me off my horse." He made me angry.

"First of all, if I wanted to kill you, you would have died, and secondly, I had to get back at you for putting my head in a pail." Smiling he shrugged as if the whole tussle had been a game.

"But why would you steal from the church? You're an angel," I asked him.

"Let's face it, with everything that has happened to you, do you really believe you would have stumbled into that place anytime soon?" He was right, I really had no desire to go back into a church.

"Oh, well, sorry about the pail then." I felt silly.

"No problem, it proved that you could hold your own." He gave me a reassuring nod.

"If it is all right with everyone, I'd just like to say that because Barnaby has his work cut out for him, we should make his job a little easier and maybe stir the pot a little every now and then to give him signs that we are around." Ariel said with a sense of mischief.

"I agree, create some sense of chaos that even evil cannot control. It will one, give us the opportunity to have some fun, if these are in fact the end of days and two, it's always nice to have a lighthouse on foreign shores." Angelo added.

"I think that is a great idea," God looked at me. "All right, it is time for you to go. I want you to know that we will be in touch, I am after all just a prayer away."

Just as I blinked, the room and everyone in it disappeared.

I woke up when the sun just began to come over the hill, Elek was sitting on a rock over me, I was laying in a pile of leaves that cushioned me from the hard ground. "You did this?" I said looking at the bed of leaves. He nodded his head. "Thanks a lot." Elek was truly a godsend, he looked after me when I needed him most.

Elek turned to something perched on top of the hill, a gated village with high walls overlooking the valley below. He pointed to it, and said with the same ancient undertone. "Find friends."

"What?" I asked. I didn't understand.

"Find friends," he said again and then with a gust of wind he returned to the pocket size statue he once was.

"You are a lot of help." I muttered sarcastically, stuffing him back into my pack. I rose from the tree line and began to trail a wagon that rattled and rolled its rickety way along the path that paralleled the brush. The single dirt road that was crudely carved into the hillside was dotted by people carrying buckets and pushing carts of fruits, furs and other goods. I didn't know how Elek expected me to make friends; in Gideon it was different. There I had help; I had no help here.

Walking cautiously into the walls of the compound I noticed that no one questioned anyone's comings or goings. Everyone just congregated around the market calmly exchanging coins for things like milk and books and handmade clothing. It was communal and refreshing to see all the faces.

Most of the buildings were just shacks made from dried dirt and twig roofs. It was simple living. As I walked through the town I noticed that the few larger buildings were either inns or pubs. Maybe if I could stay in one of these places for a night or two, I could tell someone my twisted tale and they could point me in the direction I needed to go, wherever that was.

One of the pubs stood out to me as I walked past a strip of different stores. *'Gentleman's Hyde'* was the name, its lower half was made of stone and the upper half was made from wooden beams and planks of wood running horizontally in neat parallel rows. It was one of the more permanent-looking buildings in the settlement.

As I stepped inside I smelled cigar smoke, there was also a band playing a merry song, and by the looks of it they must have been slightly drunk because they weren't completely in sync. There was no smell of warm soup like I knew from Gideon. In here all I smelled was smoked bird. I made my way to the bar, where plucked cooked turkeys hung from the ceiling, pieces ripped from the bone and placed on metal saucers. The dark wooden table seemed like it was soaked with mead and the bar stools were wobbly and creaked at the slightest touch.

I sat down and scanned the room for someone who looked approachable. I knew it would be hard to convince anyone of my story. The more I thought about it, the clearer it became that assembling a team would be improbable unless something drastic happened soon in my favor.

"That is my seat, kid." A low voice growled at me. A man, towering well over six foot, stood in front of me. His clothes were distressed and his beard was full. His bald head was home to beads of sweat as he took long drags of his cigar.

"I am sorry, I thought it was free." The man was clearly drunk, I could smell it. I didn't want a fight and I knew for a fact that it wasn't his seat. But, then again it was just a seat, so there was no point in a fuss. I got up and let the man have his seat. He sat in it and laughed; he had won some sort of personal victory in his eyes I guess.

"That was this lad's seat." Another man came up to the man and me. I was caught between them, the other man was just as big and just as mean looking, probably just as drunk.

"Well now it seems that it's mine." The man laughed as the chair creaked and shook.

The man who had apparently come to my rescue didn't like this. In fact he pushed the man off the stool and onto the ground causing his cigar to break into two and embers to go all over his shirt.

The drunk stood up and let out something that sounded like a mix between a drunken threat and a roar. He swung his fists wildly at the man and both suddenly began taking and giving punches. The whole bar for no reason at all erupted into a fight. Bottles were thrown and tables were turned over. Stools were used as weapons and I found myself running for the door.

"Oh no you don't," I was turned around on the spot. The

man who had kicked me out of my seat and the man who had apparently come to stand up for me were now standing in front of me, grabbing me by the shirt. "Night-night," one said, as both drove their fists into my face. I was knocked out cold.

"How is everything?" Michael sat directly across from me at a round table. I was in the same room I had been before, but it seemed more solemn due to the lack of company.

Both my eyes stung. I could instantly tell they were bruised and swollen. I must have been hit really hard by those men for them to knock me out like this.   "Things are okay... Where is everyone else?" I continued, knowing that Michael wouldn't care about my injuries.

"Everyone else isn't risking it," he said, annoyed.

"Risking what?" I was intrigued.

"If you haven't noticed by now, the Lennox is growing stronger. You are going to see a change pretty soon on Earth and it is not for the better. The Big Man has instructed all angels not to use any immortal power until you find them. Thus no one is here." Michael looked around the empty room.

"If God has ordered the angels into hiding, then why are you here? Shouldn't you be doing the same?" I know Michael was hardheaded, but surely he would listen to God's order.

He looked at me very matter-of-factly. "I don't hide,

it is not in my nature. Plus, someone has to help you. The little group you hope to assemble isn't going to get you through the trials you face. You won't make it to the end without my help; trust me kid, this isn't me tooting my own horn, it is a fact."

"How do you know?" I snapped. "I haven't even found anyone yet to help me."

"I can see the big picture, remember?" Michael tried to make it seem like he knew everything. "Do you know how to spot an angel who will be doing everything in their power not to be found?" He sarcastically asked. "Angels have been blending in with mankind since man first crawled up from the sea and stood on two feet, and so far man has only regarded us as good samaritans."

"Point taken." I said slumping into my chair.

"Now, let's get down to business. I called you here for a reason." Michael sat back in his chair.

"And what would that be?" Sitting up, I focused on his words.

"On your journey you will come in contact with the nine choirs. Each choir answers to God in different ways, each will help you in different ways." Michael continued. "You will first meet the Seraphim, the highest choir of the nine. Then you will progress down the line and so forth. Complete each task that is given to you and you can move on to the next. There is no room for failure."

He held out one finger and began to count. "After the Seraphim come the Cherubim, then the Thrones, Dominions, Virtues, Powers, Principalities, Archangels, and finally the Guardian angels."

"Let me get this straight. I have to not only find angels who don't want to be found but also complete ancient trials that were devised by ancient tiers created by God?" This was a little too much.

"Yes. Completion is crucial, the outcome of each task will be crucial in the plot to overthrow Lennox." Michael explained. "Don't worry. I've assigned myself to guide you, but God has left you in charge, so you must be the one to actually complete each task."

"Great," I whined.

"You got that right." Michael whined as well.

"What is the first task?" I asked after a moment of silence.

"I don't know, when we find the Seraphim they will tell us," he said, standing.

"Hey Michael." I suddenly realized something.

"Yes?"

"You listed the choirs in the order of how high they were."

"So?" He raised one eyebrow.

"Well, archangel was second to last. Doesn't that make you low on the list?" This wasn't meant to be a blow to

Michael's ego, just a simple question.

"It seems that way, yes, but you will soon see that each choir has its own place. It doesn't make any of them less important than the others; in fact the choirs benefit from the others. We all work as a machine to aid God, rather than just a jumbled assembly of higher beings, each with a different voice. That would be hectic, wouldn't it?" He shut me down with his words, and even though I hadn't meant it, I think I had just put more of a strain on our relationship.

"Any guess what the first task might be?" I said, seeing that we were in this for the long haul.

"No, but we have wasted enough time. I'll see you soon." Michael turned to the door that was on the far side of the room,

Michael opened the door letting light spill through.

My vision was blurry, I squinted as I heard a voice trying to wake me up. Even though I was laying in something soft, the aches and pulsating thumping pains made me feel like I was back on the hard pub floor.

"Where am I?" I managed.

"Oh good, you are awake. You are currently in a pile of hay." A cheerful voice let out. "My name is Nathan Porter. I live here in town. You must be new here, you don't look familiar."

"How long have I been out?" I asked.

"About two days." He sounded like it wasn't a big deal or anything.

I sat up quickly and my head began to spin.

"Careful now, you wouldn't want to get sick. Here, have some water." Nathan took out a canteen and a tiny metal cup. He carefully poured the water into the cup and then handed it to me. I drank it quickly, every last drop.

"Thanks." I said catching my breath.

"No problem." Nathan said smiling. "So tell me about yourself." He took a seat against the wall of a building next to the haystack.

"You wouldn't believe me if I told you." I said, laying back down in the hay.

"Come on, try me. Have some faith, you never know what could happen until you try it." Maybe it was the way he said it, but at that moment I knew Nathan would be the perfect person to tell my story to. It was an odd feeling, I couldn't explain it. So I told him.

We sat there for the better part of the day. He didn't ask a lot of questions; in fact he didn't ask anything. He just listened as if he cared, which made me feel like I wasn't crazy, for once.

"So that is it. I came here looking for help and as you can see I found trouble." I tried to joke about the tussle in the pub, but there was a silence that was strung tight.

Nathan looked at the ground and then at me, and then again to the ground, then back to me. "Okay." He finally said. "I will help you."

"You what?" I had hoped he would say this but I didn't

actually think he would.

"If what you say is true then how can I not come along with you? It sounds like you are on a quest to find the end of the world and I want to be apart of that. It is an adventure I'm not passing up." Nathan's tone and eyes were filled with enthusiasm and courage.

"I don't think you understand. This might be an adventure but it is nothing like a fairy tale. People have died, more will die. You will lose everything." I couldn't let him join me without knowing firsthand what would happen to him if he did. "I am a marked man, people die when they get close to me."

"And without help you will fail and what will be left for the rest of us then?" Nathan stood up and stuck out his hand to help me up. "Come on, lets see what hell we can raise."

I took his hand and was pulled to my feet. "You know for someone I just met, you sure seem really willing to help. I mean you don't even know me."

"Well, if I hadn't believed you would you still have believed in yourself?" Nathan asked.

"Yes, of course."

"Then there you have it. All you have to do is believe in yourself and others will come around. It's human instinct to follow the one who holds his head the highest. Now come on, I'll show you around." Nathan and I made our way out into the opening of the settlement where the bustling marketplace was in full swing.

"Now, this patch of land is known as the Heap, it is just your average collection of wanderers from here and there. Looking for a home, because after all everyone is just looking for a place to call their own. You will find all kinds of people here, good people, bad people, people who just want to go about their own business and so forth. Most people here live in the huts; only travelers stay in the inns above the pubs, and for good reason. As you know, it can get a little dicey in the pubs so people around here usually steer clear. Like I said before, there are good people and bad people here, but isn't that the case everywhere?" Nathan continued to show me around.

We came to a small, dirty white building with a bell tower and simple stained glass windows. One of the door handles was missing. "Over here is our little church," Nathan said. "The bell tower is used mostly for storage since the bell stopped ringing last winter. Unfortunately, not many people go to church here. It seems to have taken a back seat in many people's lives. In fact we don't even have a pastor. The only thing that keeps the church standing is a group of volunteers in town."

"Are you one of those volunteers?" I asked Nathan.

"Yes, I spent many years in the church. It has been a big part of my life." Nathan's eyes recalled memories as he spoke. "Luckily, for the both of us this works out perfectly."

"What does?" I was lost.

"I volunteer for the maintenance of this church. If you volunteer I can't pay you, but I can compensate your time with room and board." Nathan had something in store for me all along.

"Well I would need a place to stay. What did you have in mind?" I asked.

"In exchange for keeping the church presentable, you may stay in the bell tower. It isn't the most spacious of places but it will do. I will arrange for a cot and blankets to be brought up to the tower. What do you say?" Nathan's proposal was more then I could have hoped for.

"Of course," I said. "This will also give us the opportunity to recruit others to our cause."

"That's the way to think. Now, shall we continue our tour?" Nathan and I made our way past the church. We passed some more huts until we came to a tall, magnificent Victorian building. It reminded me of the Devil's dwelling. Its amber sides shined in the sun and the windows shimmered like a calm lake's surface. Rows of flowers made the bright house only brighter. There was a very positive atmosphere around it. "This is the Lawless Manor. The Lawless family owns not only the Heap but the surrounding hills and valleys. They were very successful businessmen in the South, and after the war they returned to the North and bought up a lot of the land for next to nothing. They erected the manor for their entire family to live in. Most of them didn't want to sell their businesses in the south, though, so only a few actually occupied the house.

"Over the years the Lawless family has died off and now only Mr. Lawless and his daughter Crystal live there. It's funny, all that room for two people." Nathan looked at the house with wonderment. "Sometimes Crystal will come to the church with food baskets while some of the volunteers are working. She is a sweet girl, you would like her."

"What is your story?" I asked turning to Nathan. "You know about me and you know all about this town, but you hardly have talked about yourself yet."

"There isn't much to talk about." Nathan said with a small laugh. "I am a simple man, I work most of the day and spend the rest of the time staying out of trouble." He laughed again.

"What do you do?" I asked out of curiosity.

"I am a Chaser," he replied.

"What is that?"

"In layman's terms, I am an engraver. I pretty much deal with anything from plaques to tombstones. It gets me by." Nathan shrugged and smiled.

"That's interesting, how long have you been doing that?"

"Far too long. But that isn't the important thing now. We have to get started on recruitment. Got any ideas on who you might want?" He asked.

"I don't know anyone in town, remember? I was going to ask you the same question." I didn't have the slightest clue who I was going to try and reach out to, I was actually going to leave that up to Nathan for the most part.

"I know of some people who might be willing to help. The hard part is going to be convincing them of your story. Think you can manage that?" Nathan asked.

"I'll give it my best shot." I didn't see myself as the most confident guy in the world, but I did believe in what I was fighting for and if I could get that across, I might have a chance.

"We should head back to the church. I will get you settled and we can start bright and early tomorrow." Nathan's optimism really turned things around for me. When Elek told me to make friends, I thought he was asking the impossible; but it turned out I couldn't have found a better person to start this journey with. He was understanding, kind, and most importantly, had a sense of enthusiasm and adventure that would bring so much to the table. Finding these angels and completing these tasks was not going to be an easy feat. In fact I knew I wouldn't come out of this in the same way I went into it, but with friends like Nathan I could put more then a dent in the Devil's plan.

The church was more or less a shack, as simple on the inside as the outside. A crucifix was mounted above the altar and pews flanked both sides of the room. Scattered, extinguished candles covered the floor, half of them almost completely used up. The creaky floorboards gave a slight bounce as I walked. The building definitely had character.

The bell tower was even smaller, the broken bell sat on top of a crate, my cot and sheets were neatly arranged up against one of the four walls. Luckily there were shutters to keep out the wind. Even though everything was rough around the edges, I could see this place as my home.

The time came for me to turn in. I looked out over the Heap and saw lanterns turning off one by one. Closing the shutters, I made my way over to my cot and laid down. The night dragged on. I lay awake staring blankly at the ceiling. Every so often I would blink and flashes of the past played before me like a motion picture. It was haunting. From Marshall and my parents, to Edmund, to Neo, from Gideon and Mr. Reynolds, all the way until now. I saw pools of blood form around bodies with no faces, I saw Daniel looking into my eyes before he was killed. Being in possession of the horn now, that will bring forth the Judgement was a huge responsibility. As my thoughts chased me, minutes passed in what felt like hours.

"You look like you could use some help." God was sitting on a box in the center of the room.

I sat up. "How did you get here?" I was surprised.

"Never ask how when it comes to God Barnaby, only ask when." He smiled.

"All right, when did you get here?" I asked.

"I have always been here, you just don't pay attention." He chuckled. "Now, what is disturbing you? Have I asked too much of you?" He asked, knowing the answer already.

"What is disturbing me? Are you serious? I am in over my head, everything is caving in on me and I can't dig myself out."

I had gathered information about the Devil and his forces, which gave me a huge advantage. However, I haven't gathered a team I could trust to help me in the search for the angels who were in hiding. I thought about Annabelle constantly since I had left her and the Preacher in the care of Angelo. I prayed we would meet again someday, but not during this conflict, not on the eve of battle and almost certain death. Couldn't the forces at work wait until the final drop of blood is spilled on the battle-field before she comes sweeping back into my life?

"If you can't pull yourself out, turn around and head deeper into the cave. There is always another way out." Easy for God to say, free of my mortal limitations.

"Are you really here right now?" Even though I could see Him clearly, the question still seemed relevant.

"Yes, I am. You are very different, Barnaby. So different in fact you can't begin to understand. As you are pushed and pulled in multiple directions your path will become harder. Hold fast, friend." It was good to have God close but I had to know what was so different about me.

"You're not telling me something. What is it?"

He sighed. "Let's just say I made a mistake and I am trying to fix it, but I need your help."

"*You* made a mistake?" I didn't think that was possible, at least from what I was taught. God didn't make mistakes, only miracles.

He looked at me curiously. "What? Man can say that he is only a man when he falters? But I cannot say, I am only a God?" He smiled. "My existence is different in many ways compared to that of the homosapien; I am limitless, boundless, I can flood the land and dry the seas. Extinguish the flames and freeze over the plains. But I can overlook the signs that bring thunder and rain down from a mountainside. I am just, the all powerful representation of good—but it is you who act upon nature's temptations, not I. I can only present the option of choice, while you wield the power to decide." He made sense. To a greedy mankind, the power of God is desirable.

I could see one important thing. A God was judged not by the options he presented to those He loves, but by those who expected too much from Him. When all He wanted was to give them the feeling of accomplishment by achieving it themselves.

"Man will forever be judged not by his ability to accomplish a task, but by how he tried to accomplish such a task and what he left in his wake," he added.

"Will I be remembered?" I asked, thinking of His words.

"That is man's greatest fear—not being remembered. Even the humblest think about it, but you, you will be remembered. How you want to be remembered is completely up to you. But keep this in mind, remembrance can hold heavy shackles." God looked down.

"What is Your biggest regret?" The questioned popped into my head as if it were placed there.

God looked up at me. "My biggest regret?" He paused. "I have many. Most men wish they had the ability to travel through time. To fix their mistakes and to return to the future that only exists in their dreams." He took a breath. "I have the privilege to not only to make the mistake but also to know I can go back and fix it if I wanted to."

"Then why don't you?" If God could fix anything throughout history, then there would be no wars, no plagues, no famine and no fear.

"It takes all the power of a God not to, believe me. When I am about to crumble and I lose sight of the light myself, something beyond Me reaches out and touches Me." I didn't know where He was going with this. What is beyond God?

He looked at me with glassy eyes. "Human kindness, the ability to come together, always ties up lose ends. Tragedy is a part of history, but as someone who sees it from the other side, it is the way in which we prosper. It is unity through catastrophe, when a little girl becomes an orphan, when a mother has just lost her baby in child birth, these moments are sad, yes, but it is not coincidence that the little girl's parents were pronounced dead at the same hospital that the mother lost her baby. And it is not coincidence that the nurses and doctors wear white, for everyone needs an angel when the time is right."

"What about what happened to me? With my family? Who shows up in white for me?" I said, choking up.

"There isn't a plan for everything. Even if I don't like to admit it, we must sometimes learn to improvise." God got up and placed his hand on my shoulder. "I love you, and will only be a whisper away." The room darkened and He was gone.

— Chapter Thirteen —
An Unlikely Ally

Light seeped through the shutters, filling the room. The commotion outside meant the Heap was awake and I had slept in. I had a clear agenda for what I was to accomplish. Find friends— the idea seemed simple enough. I had done it with Nathan just the day before. "Now to tell my crazy story to random strangers and look like the village loon" I said rising.

I opened the shutters and looked down to the huts and the marketplace below. People were already going about their day as if nothing was going on between Lennox and God. I wished I was one of them, oblivious.

As I closed the trapdoor and climbed down the ladder I suddenly remembered what I promised Nathan. Between the pews were supplies for fixing the church: paint cans, brushes, a screwdriver, screws, a hammer, a hand saw, nails and wooden planks all stacked neatly in the aisle. "Looks like I have my work cut out for me," I sighed. It wasn't that I didn't want to do the work on the church; I just wanted to spend the time and resources reaching out to whoever I could instead of restoring something that people hardly used.

But as the day went on I stuck to my promise. I started on the inside; after all it is what is on the inside that truly matters anyway, or so I'm told. Some of the boards from the walls were missing and needed to be replaced. I wasn't a carpenter and knew nothing of the art of building and maintaining structures. All of this was foreign to me. Then again, what was familiar in my life anymore, anyway?

One by one I drove nails into the boards to seal up the spaces. Hours passed and the light from the stained glass moved across the room. I stretched as the first on the list of many jobs came to an end. With the walls all sealed up the inside of the church was already coming together.

I walked outside to catch the last of the late afternoon sun. The marketplace was less hectic than this morning, but the Heap was still full of life as people passed and children played in the street.

"Hello there!" Nathan called, walking over to me.

"You'll be happy to know that I finished repairing the interior walls," I told him. I wanted him to know that I was thankful for everything he had done for me, and that I wasn't taking him for granted.

"Already? Wow, you must have been busy. Come on, let's get something to eat, we have a lot to talk about." Nathan and I went into a small cafe near the marketplace. It had a cozy and friendly atmosphere. We took a seat at a table out on the patio.

"Two waters and some venison steaks please," Nathan said to the waitress, after she left he turned back to me. "While you were repairing the church, I was making good use of our time as well." He pulled out a folded piece of paper.

"What is that?" I asked.

"A list of who we are going to recruit for our cause." He unfolded it proudly and cleared his throat. "Kella Hedgeridge, King and Destan Legion, and Andrew Meridius."

"Perfect, when can we talk to them?" I asked eagerly.

"Well, there is a problem." He seemed unsure of himself all of a sudden.

"What is it? I am sure we can over come it whatever it is." For the first time I found myself more confident in a situation than the other person.

Nathan sighed. "King and Kella are very, how can I say this nicely...hardheaded." He took back the list and looked it over. Gesturing to the other names, he explained.

"King's brother Destan is mute. It's unfortunate for him but also an obstacle for us, King is very protective of him. It will take a lot of convincing to get those two to join us.

"Kella is in the same boat, she has trust issues and though she is an extremely skilled huntress, she likes to be alone and doesn't play well with others." I could see why Nathan had his doubts, but he did come up with a strong list and I wasn't willing to give that up because of this hiccup. I would face this challenge like all the others, with full, unbridled force.

"What about Andrew Meridius?" I asked. Nathan hadn't mentioned him yet. Was he as difficult as the others?

"Oh, I almost forgot. Andrew is a nice guy, always has been. He will be easy to sway. His sense of spirituality is great, he believes there is always a man behind the curtain cueing the smoke and mirrors; he will see this as his one shot at getting the chance to meet that man." Nathan remarked.

After the waitress came back with our drinks and food, we discussed our next steps. I had promised Nathan that I would start to paint the inside of the church tomorrow in exchange for time with King, Destan, Kella and Andrew. He had a tricky job—if what he said about them was true, then I would definitely have my work cut out for me—but I was staying positive. I still had Nathan on my side and even though we didn't get along, I also had Michael.

Two was not enough and I wasn't going to pretend like it was. I never believed in the theory that strength only dwelled in numbers, but in this case all signs pointed in that direction.

Nathan and I parted shortly after we ate; he had some errands to run and I wanted to clean up my work station before I retired for the night. I walked into the church and noticed something was different. It was not yet dusk, but there was a candle lit on the altar. A man sat in the second row pew.

I approached him slowly, not from caution or fear, but I didn't want to startle him in the quiet that consumed the church.

"Hi, I'm Barnaby." My voice was barley above a whisper.

He turned to me slowly. He was chubby and wore rounded glasses. His brown hair was parted to the side and he looked sad, yet composed. For some reason I felt bad for him; he looked like he needed someone, a friend perhaps.

"Hi." He answered back. His voice was unsure of itself. He seemed uncomfortable but curious. "My name is Gareth."

"Mind if I take a seat?" I asked. There was something off about him, I could just tell. It was like he was a child, his demeanor just seemed to scream it.

He nodded and I joined him. We sat in silence for a few minutes; I didn't mind not talking because I think Gareth just liked having the company. He kept looking forward with a small grin on his face.

"Are you an angel?" Gareth turned to me. He asked the question like a child would ask an adult about something that was way beyond their years.

"No," I answered, then something hit me. It was like a spark lighting a powder keg. I remembered my dream, or a certain phrase from the dream: **"For you to find us, you must assemble a team to help you, each with a different strength, for it is not the job of one type of person."**

Not the job of one type of person, I thought. I looked to the single candle that flickered on the altar, then back to Gareth who was still looking at me. "I do know an angel, though."

"You do?" he asked in wonderment.

"Yes, in fact I know a lot of different angels." It was all well and good that Nathan had brainstormed and created a list of possibilities, but all of them—with the exception of Andrew—were the same. King and Destan were close-knit brothers and they were strong, Kella was strong and a huntress with a lack of trust.

173

But then there was Gareth. He gave off a sense of innocence and wonderment. He was something that our cause needed; he was the reason that we were fighting. We were fighting for the good, for the ones who couldn't stand alone. "Would you like to hear a story Gareth?" I asked him. He nodded and I began to describe my journey.

The entire time Gareth's attention was fixed on me. He devoured every word and hung onto every detail. At the end he even clapped. "You did all that?" he asked.

I laughed a little. To me it was just a bizarre twist of fate, but to him I was like a knight in shining armor riding up to him and asking him for his autograph. He was stunned.

"Yes sir, and if you want to, you can come along and help me finish finding the angels."

He reacted instantly. "You mean it? I can really come with you?"

Gareth was thrilled and practically jumped out of his seat. Two things raced through my mind at the thought of Gareth joining our team: One, our numbers were growing and I was starting to see the value of a person's compassion over physical ability. Two, this would put Gareth in a lot of danger, I wasn't sure if he could handle all of this. Nonetheless I wouldn't go back on my word.

"When are we going to meet the angels?" he asked excitedly.

"Well, first we have to gather more people to make our

trip easier. Then it will only be a matter of time before we come across one." This blanket response was enough to make it look like I knew what I was doing.

"All right, I'll see you tomorrow." Gareth got up happily and left the church with a hop in his step. It made me feel good that he was filled with such purpose.

Extinguishing the candle, I cleaned up the nails and wood from earlier. I climbed back up into the bell tower and laid down on the cot. I was tired from the day's work but fulfilled all the same. If Nathan and I could recruit the list he had come up with and find some others who were less likely to be heroes in the eyes of a stereotype, like Gareth, then maybe we could show others that people could stand together from different ends of the spectrum.

"Two will not be sufficient. No matter how you rationalize." Michael sat across from me at the table in the empty room where we had met before.

"I believe in who I have brought on. For you to challenge their worth before meeting them does not show your strength but your lack of vision." I fired right back. He had no knowledge of Nathan or Gareth and he only measured men by physical worth, not their strength of spirit.

"That is not what I meant." Michael's expression changed.

"What did you mean then?" I still wasn't giving him an inch. In my opinion he was as judgmental as they come.

"You have gotten off to a good start. However, the ones who you have enlisted will not withstand the battery of this task. More must be gathered to overcome the numbers you will face. One man can yell from the rooftops, two men can raise hell, yet three or four men can wave a banner and lift up the populace."

Suddenly I got it. It wasn't that he didn't believe in what I had done, he was just suggesting in his own way how to improve and build upon what I already had.

"You see Barnaby, I am on your side. We both have a common goal and if we intend on reaching it we have to face the facts and work together. At this point I am your only hope in locating the other angels anytime soon. When the time comes I will appear to you and that is when we will get started." We had come to the conclusion that we don't have to like each other but we do have to fight side by side, maybe even back to back to accomplish what God has entrusted us to do.

"I understand. What are we going to do?" I asked. "And don't give me the same answer that I have to come up with that on my own because I am sick of hearing it." That was all I heard during these discussions. Was there no way that they could help me?

"I am not like the others. I am not going to sugarcoat anything. My advice, if you want to take it, is to keep doing what you're doing. Restore the church, learn from the work you put into it and you may be surprised by what comes from caring." This was the most advice I had been given, yet it was still mysterious.

"What are you going to do in the meantime?" I asked, wondering where Michael saw himself in all of this.

"Like I said, when the time is right I will find you. Now go. We will not meet here again." Michael got up and walked over to the door. "The next time I see you it will be in person. Good luck and stay focused." He put his hand on the doorknob and before I could say anything else, he opened it and light poured in.

— Chapter Fourteen —

His Cross to Bear

I opened my eyes. Nathan was standing over my bed with a smile. It was sort of creepy in a way, but I didn't feel threatened. "Yes?" I moaned, stretching as I sat up.

"Good morning." He was particularly jolly this morning. I wonder why?

"Good morning to you too." I yawned.

"Guess who agreed to meet with you?" Now I knew why he was so happy.

"Who?" From the conversation I'd had with Michael the night before, it didn't matter who was agreeing to meet with me. I saw everyone as an asset.

"You were supposed to guess. Anyway, Andrew agreed to meet with us near the market, isn't that great? Hey, it's a start." He shrugged, but I saw no negative in our situation.

"Doesn't matter. The others will come around eventually." Nathan and I both smiled and climbed down the ladder to the church.

"By the way, nice job with the walls. The place looks better than ever." Nathan laughed and continued out the door.

I looked around and thought of Michael's words:

"Restore the church, learn from the work you put into it and you may be surprised by what comes from caring."

"Barnaby, come on!" Nathan called from outside, I followed.

He was in a hurry and so was I. We both didn't want to keep Andrew waiting. I hadn't told Nathan about Gareth yet; I figured I would wait until after we talked to Andrew.

"Hello Andrew!" Nathan called out over the crowd.

A tall man in homemade clothing stood still among the rushing people. He was slim and had brown hair, grey eyes, and a charming smile. He looked to be of Spanish descent. "Nathan, good to see you," he called back as he walked over. "My name is Andrew Meridius, and you are?" He stuck out his hand in a welcoming manner.

"Barnaby Maverick." I firmly shook his hand and we exchanged a brief smile. Andrew turned to Nathan. "So what was it that you wanted to talk about?"

Nathan turned to me. I guess this was my time to shine. "Actually, I had asked Nathan if I could meet with you." I interjected. "I have a story I would like to share with you."

"A story? I think I have time to hear a good story." Andrew laughed. "Let's get a round of drinks and discuss." Nathan and I followed him to the closest pub, called *Never More*. The pub's interior was almost identical to the *Gentlemen's Hyde*. though surprisingly crowded for the time of day. We still managed to get a table in the corner of the room. Nathan went up to the bar to get the drinks, leaving us alone.

"This doesn't have to deal with dragons and wizards, does

it? Because if it does I really don't want to waste my time." Andrew admitted.

"No, but keep an open mind nonetheless." I gulped, thinking that I might have overestimated Andrew's willingness to believe what I was about to tell him.

Nathan came back with the drinks and set them on the wooden table, I reached for one of the mugs and took a rather large gulp from it straight away. "Easy there Barnaby, it is still early in the day." Nathan joked.

"Sorry," I croaked wiping my mouth with my sleeve.

"Now what was it that you wanted to talk to me about?" Andrew asked taking a sip of the foamy liquid.

"It isn't easy to explain, so I will just come right out and say it." I took another swig and continued. "I have traveled a great distance and I have stumbled through obstacles that some would call fantasy."

"I thought I said I didn't want my time wasted with wizards and dragons." Andrew raised an eyebrow at me.

"Let him finish—I am sure you will think differently at the end." Nathan intercepted.

"No, not dragons and not wizards. But, angels and demons. A God and a vengeful Devil." I looked at Andrew trying to predict whether or not he was going to walk out on me right then and there.

Something in his eyes told me that he was intrigued, that he could possibly be convinced after all. I had to play my hand well now if I was going to keep it this way. "Angels you say? Go on." He said sipping his drink.

"All right, it all started some months ago. I was in a rut, like all men are when they have hit rock bottom. I was blinded to faith and saw things in a way which I know they aren't now; one dimensional, one sided, predictable, merciless."

Everything was coming back to me, I felt very comfortable talking to both Nathan and Andrew, like I was destined to have this conversation.

"I had collapsed both mentally and physically, and I felt like I was thrown down into a well. With everything that had happened to me I was still too thick-headed to ask for help. It is funny looking back at it now, a man with nothing found on the floor still had too much pride to take the hand extended to him. But, then again, a man with nothing holds on to what pride he has, for that is all that accompanies him at night. Even so, I was given help by two strangers, two friends."

As my story went on, none of us touched our drinks. In the beginning I was nervous about Andrew's reaction. I considered myself cursed with the responsibility to carry out the fall or ultimate rise of Lennox; from what I gathered from the angels, it was mostly up to me.

At the end of my tale Andrew was silent and so was Nathan. This time around when I told the story I recalled more of the emotions and details that were associated with it. I didn't sugarcoat it like I did when I told Gareth.

"That is what is brewing in the back round." Nathan said gently, breaking the silence.

Andrew smiled and drank from his mug. "I don't doubt your story. You know Barnaby, it has always interested me how human life is intertwined in all of this." Andrew waved his index finger in the air symbolizing the universe. "What you told me is my life's wonderment come to life. Everything has a purpose and I have found mine in it all, what a wonderful feeling." He lifted his mug and we did the same. "Here comes the light my friends." As we toasted and drank the bar livened up in a way which didn't seem friendly. Arguments sprang up like tantrums from toddlers who didn't want to share their toys.

"This doesn't look good." Nathan said putting his mug down.

"Let's get out of here." I suggested.

"I agree." Andrew got up and gestured for us to do the same. The door was on the other side of the room, practically right through the crowed of disgruntled drunks.

"Play it cool and we should be out of this in no time." Nathan appeared calm. However, there was a slight quiver in his voice. I didn't know him for long, but from what I gathered, he wasn't exactly a fighter.

"You're a cheat!" yelled one of the men in a slurred sound.

"You are drunk old man, I had the better hand! Now pay up!" A man who was built like a wall barked.

"You won he lost, give it a rest already." One of the

sympathizers for the old man stepped forward.

"Stay out of this," he snapped. "I want the money, what good is a man if he can't hold a bet." The tension in the small room brewed like a boiling pot that was ready to blow its lid. Nathan, Andrew and I couldn't get out of there fast enough. Some other folk had the same idea for they too were making their way towards the door.

"No one is leaving, no one is coming." Another man came into the picture, he stood in front of the door and flexed his arms. He was at least twice the size of the rest of us and he was all brute and business.

From out of the dark corner a bottle flew right into the side of the large betting man's head. Everyone in the bar froze as he let out a yell.

"I would suggest taking cover," Andrew stated.

As chairs began to fly in all directions we bolted back to the corner table. Diving across it we found ourselves cornered in an all-out brawl. Bottles smashed, chairs began to splinter, tables turned, everything and everyone was chaotic.

"Is there any other way out of here?" I said over the noise.

"Not unless you want to hurl yourself through a window." Andrew joked. "Just stay calm and keep your head down, this will all be over soon. Fights like this never last, you'll see, drunks have a tendency of wearing themselves out."

From upstairs came a loud thump. It was the sound of a door slamming shut. There must have been an inn upstairs and one of the residents was coming to see what all the commotion was about.

"That isn't good." Nathan looked up at the ceiling.

"What isn't good?" I asked, wondering how any of this could get any worse.

"This isn't *Never More* is it?" Andrew asked, looking up at the ceiling as well.

"I am afraid it is, my friend." Nathan and Andrew both knew something I didn't and it was starting to worry me.

Nathan turned to me with a worried glance. "Brace yourself, Barnaby."

Slowly, in between the breaking of bar stools and bottles was the sound of footsteps on the creaky stair case. I peered over the table and saw a girl with a high, long, brown ponytail. She had slender features and though she was small she was all muscle. She showed little emotion but underneath that almost expressionless face was a snarl. In an instant the slicing of air cut through the room and the man who started all this, was struck with an arrow in the chest. He screamed and fell to the ground. Everyone stopped and in an instant the fight was over. However, Nathan and Andrew both advised me to stay down.

"You, you could have killed me." The man gasped trying to pull the arrow from his now bleeding chest.

"If I wanted you dead you would be dead. What is done is done so don't cry about it. Also, don't pull that out; it's better to leave those sort of things in till someone more qualified than a drunken oaf can look at it." She looked around.

"Now which one of you disturbed my nap." She said slowly taking out another arrow and placing it on the bow.

No one moved and no one dare speak. The old drunken man pointed to the man with the arrow in his chest. The girl smirked. "Of course he did, all right get out, the lot of you." Without question everyone made their way to the door. When they did however, they were stopped by the man who had been blocking it.

"I said no one was to leave and I don't care if you think otherwise, sweetheart."

"Oh dear." Nathan said with a hushed voice, we were still hiding behind the corner table and at that moment I was glad we were.

"You want to guard the door then fine, guard the door. But never, ever call me sweetheart again." She pushed her way through the crowed and kicked the man in the stomach as hard as she could knocking him backwards. He slammed against the door, causing it fly off its hinges. The man and the door were now both outside. The girl smirked just a tiny bit and vacated the pub. Everyone else followed except for the three of us, who stood there alone in an empty, disheveled room.

"Who was that?" I let out standing up.

"That, that was Kella Hedgeridge." Andrew blankly stated.

"Kella Hedgeridge? The Kella Hedgeridge? The one you wanted me to talk to?" I was shocked. She hardly seemed open-minded or even approachable, for that matter.

"Maybe we can catch up to her." Nathan must have been off his rocker.

"What? You want to go after her? After what we just witnessed? That could have been us." I didn't see Nathan's reasoning.

"Of course, we should go after her. We know firsthand what she can do and that is exactly why we need her. Now come on." Andrew and I followed Nathan out the door.

I was more than a little worried at what might happen. The best possible outcome was that she had calmed down enough to hear me out. The questions swirled in circles; what if she snaps again? What if I am knocked out for the second time since I've been here? What if she laughs in my face when I ask if she will help me, will she even give me the chance to hear what I have to say? I didn't want to find any of these questions out. Something told me it wasn't going to go over well.

"Come on, I think she went this way." Nathan continued to lead us across the Heap.

"We can always come back and try another day, can't we?" I pleaded. The look on Andrew's face was that of agreement for he too didn't seem completely comfortable with the idea. Even though he and Nathan both saw the potential in Kella, I couldn't get past the notion that she might not be a team player and that was the last thing we needed to deal with.

Nathan led us to an alleyway on the eastern side of town.

"I think she went down this way," he said as he entered the deserted alley.

"Nathan, I think Barnaby may be right, this doesn't feel right." Andrew spoke up with concern. For Kella to stir unease in both of us, made me realize even more that we needed her. I didn't want to admit it but it was fact. I had to muster the courage to speak with her. What was the worst that could happen? I was in the company of Nathan and he was unfazed, so why shouldn't I be?

"If you think she went this way there is only one way to find out." I forced myself to say. Taking the first step was hard, taking the next was near impossible. There was a feeling of hesitation but I pressed on. I looked back to Nathan and Andrew, who followed close behind me. Their eyes darted everywhere.

With a gust of wind I left the ground. I found myself swinging back and forth with the world upside down. My foot was caught in a snare that was set moments before probably by Kella. I had walked into a trap.

"Well, Nathan?" I said, finding this whole mess his fault. I wasn't mad at him, I was just frustrated at the fact that whenever something happened, I was usually the one who was caught up in the middle of it all.

"Who are you?" I heard the stern voice of Kella from the other end of the alley. With my back turned to her I couldn't see whether or not she had her bow drawn. I hoped she didn't, she did after all shoot a man for simply waking her.

"Hello Kella." Nathan stepped to the side of me to make himself seen. "This is Barnaby Maverick. He is a friend of mine and I was hoping we could have a moment of your time?" Nathan got straight to the point on this one, he was a little nervous but held it together.

"I don't want to hear anything that he has to say." Kella answered without giving it much thought at all.

"Just hear him out. I did, and it is something we must all concern ourselves with." Andrew stood behind Nathan in order to not become a target.

"I don't have to concern myself with anything. None of you are worth my time, my attention or my curiosity. Now untie your friend and leave before I have to humiliate you further." This was probably the only opportunity I was going to get to talk to Kella, but I recognized the call of retreat when it sounded and knew that if there was a will there would be a way, it would just have to happen another time.

"We should listen to her before anything else happens to me. Besides, we have time." I recommended before Nathan could protest.

"All right Kella, you win." Nathan was clearly disappointed. "Come on Andrew, help me untie him." Andrew and Nathan freed me from the snare and I fell to the ground.

"Sorry about that." Andrew and Nathan helped me up and brushed the dirt off my hoodie. "All right, let's get something to eat and we can talk about how we are going to go about the delicate task of not getting killed." Andrew suggested.

"Agreed," both Nathan and I said simultaneously.

I still hadn't told them about Gareth. I thought I'd wait until I got everyone under one roof; this way it would be too late for debate. This was going behind their backs, but for the time being I felt compelled to gather a diverse group of volunteers, not just those with brute strength or wit.

We left the alley empty handed. Kella completely rejected even the thought of entertaining our request to speak with her. Perhaps she wasn't meant to join us, maybe it was for the best.

As we sat down in the cafe we all had the look of disconnected concentration, all within our own little thought bubbles. My mind wasn't attached to the subject of gathering people, it was attached to the church. Come to think of it, all day I was thinking of the church and ways in which to improve it. I had some infatuation with it now, like it was a part of my mission.

"What we have to do is consider broadening this list. We can't just select these individuals, we won't get anywhere, especially with their temperaments." Andrew was going over the list Nathan had so thoughtfully scribbled down. "I have no doubt that we will eventually need them to progress, however for now we convince the dreamers, the hopeful, the ones who have nothing and search for something to hold. They will be our structure, our skeleton. Then and only then will we be able to gain the muscle." When Andrew spoke he did so almost poetically. It reminded me of the way the angels spoke.

"I can see now that I perhaps bit off more than I could chew. We have to work from the bottom and raise ourselves to great heights. Accomplishing this can only mean one definite route." When Nathan spoke it was like he was a passionate tactician. He recognized and realized the strength within the elements we possessed that others around him might not have noticed. His mind was open to possibilities that might be considered fiction and more importantly he could admit when he was wrong. "Gentlemen," he looked at us and smiled. "Look at this from the standpoint of what's meant to be will be. What I mean is that the ones who wish to follow, will follow. The ones who don't wish, simply won't. Let our attention not be drawn to them but on finding the angels."

"I couldn't have said it better myself." When the time comes I know we will be prepared. How could I have any doubt about that when I had friends like these?

It was just around dusk when I returned to the church. Gareth was patiently waiting outside. "Hi Barnaby!" He waved and smiled.

"Hi Gareth, what are you doing here?" I didn't mind that Gareth was here, I actually enjoyed his company but still, I was curious.

"I just thought I would stop by." He said swaying.

"You are more than welcome to visit. How is everything?" I opened the church doors and we both went inside.

"Great. I've been thinking." Gareth was excited in his

tone.

"Oh? About what?" I was intrigued.

Gareth cleared his throat. "You said you needed friends to help you with your adventure. I think I have a way to do just that."

"Really? How?" Any help after what just happened with Kella would be nice.

"By throwing a party." Gareth had all the best intentions in mind but I don't think he grasped the concept of what we were doing here. "Everyone loves a good party and its a great way to share stories and laughs and make new friends." He was smiling ear to ear. A lot of planning had gone into this idea.

"I wish it was that simple, Gareth." I smiled.

"No party then?" Gareth sat down on a pew; he didn't look too happy.

"Now, I didn't say that." I didn't want to hurt his feelings. He meant well and the idea wasn't completely outlandish. "I'll tell you what, we will have a party when I finish fixing the church, how does that sound?" If I could finish restoring the church with Gareth's help, then I could not only complete my end of the bargain that I have with Nathan, but also I could devote all of my efforts into the immense task that lay ahead.

"You mean it? We can have one?" Gareth suddenly sat up on the bench.

"Of course, we can even throw it here." I couldn't help but smile. I sensed he didn't have joyous occasions often and that saddened me. He had a good soul, a kind spirit. I envied him for this and hoped others would take notice and mimic such an uncommon attribute.

"That sounds delightful. Can I help you finish?" The positive nature of Gareth made me forget all about our run-in with Kella today.

"I wouldn't want to have it any other way." The room was beginning to grow darker. "For tonight, however, I think we both need to rest. Tomorrow you can come by and I will have a job all set up for you, how does that sound?" I was happy that Gareth was helping with the church, not just because it would be nice to have a helping hand, but because I think it would be good for him and honestly it would be good for me as well.

"Okay, that sounds fine." With that Gareth got up and walked out the door.

I climbed the latter and went through the trap door that led to the bell tower. Opening the shutters I looked out on the Heap. Just like the night before, lights were extinguished one by one by the ones who were drowsy. Out of the corner of my eye was the lit up manor that the Heap was built around. It was grand and spectacular compared to the simplicity of everything else around it. To think only two people lived there boggled my mind, although they did come from the south where comforts like that might just be a standard of living.

"Hello, Barnaby." I turned around on a dime. God was sitting next to the broken church bell on a crate looking at me. He looked tired but he smiled nonetheless.

"God? What are You doing here?" Michael had told me that it was too dangerous for any of them to be caught out like this.

"I wanted to talk with you. I am sure you have some questions." I was surprised and grateful to see Him.

"I don't think we have time for all the questions I have for You." I joked.

"Then let's start with the ones that are most relevant to here and now." He was level headed, something I needed to be.

"See, that is where the problem lies. I don't know what is here and now, what is relevant, what is important to know and what is just a waste of time." There always seemed to be a fork in the road and I always wasted time wondering which path I should go down. When I did choose, I would spend my time walking down the path wondering if it was the right choice after all.

"Then I will ask, for I have questions too." God had questions?

"You want to ask me a question?" I really couldn't believe my ears.

"From time to time even I do wonder. Does this surprise you?" God looked at me with one eyebrow slightly raised.

"I figured You, out of all people would know what to do all the time. Isn't that what being You is all about?" I was always told that no matter the uncertainty, no matter the situation, God always had a plan and everything would just come to be.

"May I confide something in you, Barnaby?" God asked.

"Sure." The air was still.

"I am everything and anything. I see what can't be seen and I can stop what can't be undone, I have what the human race calls power, unlimited some might suggest. This is true to an extent. I have access to what is unknown in the universe, I am apart of the Father, the Son and the Holy Ghost."

God stood up. "All of this I wield with word, with love, with compassion and yes sometimes with silence. For it is not just to answer every call to demonstrate what I am to the masses." He now paced the tiny room. "Barnaby, I will let you in on a little secret, something that I believe will help you in the future. When creation began, before both Adam and Eve, I made one living being that I can truly say captured my heart. She was my greatest creation, her spirit merged with that of every rock and every stream, every leaf and every reef. Her name was Earth. She took all life and cradled it in her arms, taking care of its needs, helping it grow and making sure the delicate balance continued through day and night. I on the other hand stayed back and watched down upon her and all of our children, only to direct when needed, for I have faith that every heart will do what is right."

"Just like the mother stays to watch over her children, the father returns only when needed to protect or supply what is necessary for life. Thus, that is why I am called the Father and the Earth is called the Mother." God turned to me. "That is my role Barnaby, to take the immense power I have and condense it, to discipline it so that things like the Earth, love, acceptance, peace and free will may not be forced upon anyone. An object will thrive when it believes it can on its own and of course when it is ready. So until I am absolutely needed, I will stay on the sidelines like a proud parent, for when one is needed that is when one will be called. Do you understand?"

"No," I said looking up at God and blinking.

"Good, that is the answer I wanted to hear. It isn't for you to understand just yet." God smiled and patted me on the head. "Now, I don't want you going around thinking my absence means I am not present, it only means that I follow, unless of course I am invited to walk beside, then I am honored." He winked. "Keep that in mind the next time you find yourself alone. Promise?"

"Promise." I hadn't quite gotten what God was trying to tell me; it wasn't every day I took in this kind of information and processed it. However, He did say it wasn't for me to understand just yet so I held onto what might possibly be a saving grace later on.

God smiled at me once more and looked out the window into the night sky. There was a full moon tonight. "I must go, goodnight. Tomorrow is another day." With another blink I was left alone in the room, the shutters rattled in the breeze and my eyes began to grow weary. I laid on my cot and quickly drifted away.

Chapter Fifteen

The Iron Man's Rust

Dreams—they had become a double-edged sword. On one hand they gave me peace that I wasn't alone in the middle of this struggle. That there were angels to guide me, once I found them of course. On the other hand they haunted me; the very angels that appeared in them became mile markers or cornerstones in a campaign that I had little control over.

"I am here Barnaby!" Gareth opened the door to the church. He had a lunch pail and was swinging it joyfully as he crossed the room.

"Hey Gareth, be careful. The walls have wet paint on them." Gareth stopped and looked around.

"Oh okay, I'll be careful then." He said putting his lunch pail on one of the pews. "I made you a ham sandwich," he said opening the metal box exposing two sandwiches.

"That was very kind of you. What do you say? Want to help me paint?" I asked holding out a second brush. "Sure, I like to paint." He smiled.

We painted into the afternoon and took a short break to enjoy the sandwiches Gareth had brought. The church was looking better and better and as it did I felt better as well. I had come to a place that had welcomed me, I made friends and I had found a home. It was great and I would keep these things in the back of my mind during the battles ahead to remember what I was fighting for. Not what the world needed, but what I, Barnaby Maverick, needed.

"Excuse me." A sweet tone swept through the room. It didn't disturb the silence but gently set it aside. Gareth and I both turned away from the paint-covered walls to see where it had come from.

"Hi Crystal!" he shouted, plopping the brush into the bucket and making his way over to her.

"Well hello Gareth, are you working hard?" She smiled at him, holding a basket that had various fruits and snacks inside.

Her smile was breathtaking and bright, welcoming and soothing. It was instantly disarming and nurturing, filling the room with wonderment and innocence. I was lost in the pools of her bright blue eyes that swirled in circles. Her blonde hair lined up with her fair skin; she wasn't very tall but her laugh was bubbly and filled with charm and grace.

"Hello." She was standing right in front of me. I must have been daydreaming or something because I didn't see her approach me. She was looking at me with a slight sense of confusion. She must have been trying to get my attention.

"Sorry, hi, my name is Barnaby Maverick." I quickly stuck out my hand, hitting her in the stomach with it.

Right as I hit her she dropped the basket causing all the fruit and snacks to fall out. She fell to ground and looked up at me. "Well nice to meet you too." She didn't sound surprised or hurt or even mad. I dropped to the ground and immediately started apologizing. I swiftly began picking up everything that had fallen and began putting it back into the basket.

"Want to help me up?" She asked looking at me with the eyes that drove me from paying attention to begin with.

"Uh, sure, no problem." I stood up placing the basket on one of the pews.

As I helped her up I felt my cheeks begin to blush. When she got to her feet we stood there face to face, inches apart, looking into each other's eyes as if nothing else around us existed.

"You are blushing." She said diverting her eyes and tucking a strain of hair behind her ear.

"I just feel bad about what happened." I looked away too.

"The name is Crystal Lawless." Meeting my eyes again she extended her hand.

"I heard about you." I answered shaking it.

"Only good things I hope." She smiled.

"Crystal, you have to hear Barnaby's story!" Gareth called out.

"I don't think she wants to be bothered." I tried to change the subject.

"Nonsense." She sat down on the pew next to the basket. "I am all ears."

Trying to back out now wasn't going to work, Crystal stared at me with attentiveness and Gareth with much anticipation. "All right, fine." I said, taking a seat on top of a pile of wood. "Some time ago, on my travels…"

I told the story and as I did Gareth called out about certain details being his favorite parts. Crystal tilted her head ever so slightly every once in a while but remained completely silent until finally, I finished.

"What did you think?" Gareth burst out straightaway.

"That is certainly some story." I couldn't tell if Crystal thought I was mental or not. It was a crazy thing to hear from a stranger who had accidentally punched her in the stomach just moments before. If I were her, I would have thought there might be something off about me.

"Barnaby and I are going on an adventure!" Gareth announced.

"Oh?" Crystal looked from him to me. "You are taking him on this trip?"

"Yep, Nathan Porter and Andrew Meridius agreed to come along as well." I added.

"You have quite a following there." Crystal appeared unsure of what to say.

"I hope you don't think I'm crazy. Everything I said is true, and what I told you isn't even the worst of it." I rambled on.

Crystal stood up and walked over to me. She took my hands and held them in hers. "I don't think you are crazy, I believe you."

"You do?" Her sincerity was clear.

Smiling, she cleared up any question I had.

"When are we leaving again?" Gareth asked, leaning forward.

"I am not sure, soon though." That was something I hadn't given much thought to. I was told to gather as many people as I could, however I wasn't told when to act.

"As long as we are prepared for when the time comes it shouldn't really matter. In the meantime let's finish cleaning up this place, we have a lot to do." Crystal suggested as she picked up a paint brush.

I don't know if meeting Crystal was an act of divine plan or if it was just coincidence, but whatever the reason I was happy it happened. She had a certain spunk about her that I knew would round out our motley crew. With Nathan, Andrew, Gareth, and now Crystal I was becoming more and more comfortable with the fact that any day now I will be fighting a war that was going to change the course of human history.

We worked for a few more hours. The basket of food Crystal had brought by was shared between the three of us as we talked about this and that and the road ahead.

"Well, I think that is enough for today." Crystal announced. "All work and no play is not okay, now come on." Crystal wiped her hands and picked up the now-empty basket. She began to walk towards the door then turned around. "Come on now, while the sun is still high." She smiled and looked at me. "Barnaby, you have to enjoy life and live a little to fight for it."

"There is still a lot to do with the church and I made a

promise to finish it." I tried telling her.

"I have an idea!" Gareth shouted.

"Yes?" Crystal and I both said with a slight laugh.

"Why don't you two go have fun and I will finish up
here?" Gareth was very kind, he put others before him.

"That is very sweet Gareth, but you deserve a break too."
Crystal's tone was gentle; she too saw the innocence of Gareth's
offer and appreciated it.

"No, no, no, I won't have it. Now, go on." Gareth brushed
us to the door. He was determined.

We stepped outside and the door was closed behind us,
Crystal looked at me and I looked at her. "Well, I guess that settles
it" she said, laughing.

I smiled back. "So, you have me out here, what now?" I
was still new here and I only knew a handful of people.

"I figured we could get some air," she suggested.

"Okay?" I didn't know what she meant. It wasn't like the
church was stuffy.

She giggled at my confusion. "Come on, I'll show you
what I mean." Taking me by the hand we made our way through
the Heap. In minutes we came to a fairly large building. It was a
stable.

"Get it now?" She said gesturing to the building.

"We are going for a ride?" I asked. "But why?"

"Because, you have been fixing that church all day and
need to get out." She was right about me working on the church

all day, but I didn't have time to be riding horses for leisure. I had to finish the church and find some way to contact the first angel.

"I really appreciate whatever you are trying to do, but I have to go back and finish what I started. Thanks anyway." I had to deny Crystal's invitation, I had a job now, a job that was consuming my life and wouldn't be completed until either I died or evil was vanquished, if that was even possible.

"What, you can't ride?" She poked fun at me. I grew a little irritated. I was aware of the situation that surrounded us more than anyone else because I lived it. It was just a story to everyone else, something they could either accept to believe or not. But for me, it wasn't a choice to believe or not. I lived through it all.

"No I can, that isn't the point." My voice was harsher now but I was still calm.

"Then what is it?" she said.

"I told you. The angels and demons are fighting and I'm stuck in the middle. I don't have time for this. I am sorry I can't be sidetracked, I just can't afford it right now." I was spent. I had kept this in but I couldn't anymore. I just couldn't find the strength to laugh along as if I was unaware.

In that moment I wanted to just drop everything and head out on this journey alone. I wondered if I would be better off, I wondered how long I would last. Would the company of others really make a difference? Death loomed over me like vultures following soldiers into battle. Did I really want to wish that on the others? No, I didn't; all I wanted was for all of this to be over, and if that meant that I had to die in the process, than I would be totally fine with that. Bury me under a tree by a brook and forget the whole thing happened.

"You're still wrapped up in that? Barnaby, everything will align in its place, don't stop for a second because you think you have to change who you are all of a sudden. God picked you because He knew you could handle it, so why go changing what He saw as a strength in the first place?" What grabbed me about Crystal's statement was the truth behind it. She understood and she explained it in a way I wouldn't have. She was the one looking in through the glass, watching what was happening and relaying the message.

We stood in silence. I couldn't look at her. Instead I glanced at the stable. I thought about what she said for a moment and realized something that was lurking under the surface. From the point of being made aware of this war, I had constantly lived in fear, I feared for the ones around me, I feared for the next steps I took and for the consequences of my actions. Everything that was haunting me suddenly suffocated me. But no more, no more will I be cornered by this notion. Sure, I may die tomorrow or even later today. However, this life is still mine and I will live how I wish to be remembered.

Without so much as a glance towards Crystal, I started to walk away from her.

"Barnaby? Barnaby, where are you going?" Crystal's voice trailed behind me.

I walked into the stable through one of the side doors. The five horses that were in there looked at me blankly. "Hello fellas." I said as I grabbed a saddle. "All right, who is it gonna be?" I asked looking around. Then I saw it, a beautiful, brown horse with a flowing brown mane, but what struck me most were the various splotches of white it had across its body.

I had never saddled a horse, but I had seen it done once before. Luckily, the horse I chose was very calm and patient. Once the straps were all secure I jumped up and assessed the situation. "All right, Barnaby. Forget everything you have ever worried about. Let the wind strip away any thought of failure, in this moment you are free from your demons." It must have been silly to be talking to myself but it actually gave me some relief.

The horse nudged the stable's doors open with its head and walked outside. Crystal looked at me and smiled. "I knew you could do it." I couldn't have done it without her.

Giving a slight kick, the horse took off towards the main gate of the Heap. Once outside I felt like I was in the middle of nowhere and I liked it. Everything was so refreshing and each breath felt like my first. It didn't even hit me that I had left Crystal in the dust. Slowing down, I stopped and waited for her to catch up.

"Thanks for waiting up!" she joked, riding up to me on a black and white horse.

"Sorry," I said.

"Don't worry about it." She smiled.

We both were at a trot now. I took a deep breath and looked up at the sky. It was the time of day where the stars and moon could be seen but the sun was still in the sky. "When I was little, this would be my favorite time of day. My mother would tell me and my brother that it was when the sun, moon and stars would come together in harmony. This particular time of day is rare and special because it can only happen on the clearest of days and it is only visible for a brief period of time. She also told us that during this time, everything would be good in the world because it is when the life that has departed lifts up and dries up the misfortunes of those who have fallen on hard times." I don't know why I had broken the silence to tell Crystal this, but I just couldn't help but recall the memory.

"That's beautiful. You seem like you had a good relationship with your family." She sounded curious like she wanted to hear more about them, I wasn't sure whether or not I wanted to bring them up. It was like burning a candle at both ends when it came to them, eventually I would have to say what happened.

"Yeah, we were close." I looked back up at the sky.

Luckily, Crystal had taken the hint when I said we **were** and she didn't continue the conversation.

"Hey, you want to get off here and just sit a while?" Crystal pointed to a clearing in the tall grass.

"Sure," I responded, still in a dreamlike state. Seeing the sky this way reminded me of Marshall and my mother and father.

Dismounting, we walked into the field to the clearing that Crystal had pointed out. The air was crisp and the grass was cool.

"When I get stressed, I come out here to the meadow to sit and just relax." Crystal sat on the ground and took a deep breath, then exhaled. "See? It is that simple." Crystal's optimism was a foreign feeling but none the less she got me out here so I was willing to give it a shot.

Taking a seat next to her, I looked back up at the sky. "You know, I think this is working."

"Yeah?" She smiled like her mission was accomplished.

"Yeah, for the longest time I always looked at the glass as half empty. I always felt like no matter what I did I couldn't catch a break. But now, I feel kind of at peace." I took a breath. I was feeling what I never thought I could feel, relief. My family was still on my mind but sadness didn't surround their memories now, only a sense of harmony, the same harmony that my mother talked about when the sun, moon and stars came together. "Hey Crystal."

"Yes Barnaby?" She looked at me as she played with the ends of her dress.

"Do you think it is crazy to think somewhere out there, someone is looking out for you and keeping you safe?" I laid back and began counting the stars.

"Of course not, I mean there is always someone out there who loves you. Even if you feel like you're alone, remember, there is always someone thinking about you." She laid back too.

"Let's just say if someone was the last person alive in their family. Is it fair to assume that someone out there is there for them?" To think that my family was out there looking out for me was a dream, they were gone and even though I could surround myself with people, I just couldn't seem to fill the gap they had left.

Crystal's hand reached down and held mine. It was a weird feeling; the connection between us was something I couldn't quite explain. Emotions pulsed through me as my mind tried to make sense of it. I felt our heartbeats connect like we were somehow syncing to each other. I looked at her and she looked at me, the light in her blue eyes swirled like ripples on a glassy pond. "Family are those who stay by your side. Those who you love unconditionally and those who you fight for. Don't say you're alone because of the limitations of physical connection. You are exactly where you are supposed to be." I didn't know what to say. She was right, again. It seemed that Crystal knew exactly what to say; she was something special.

"Of course family can be a pain sometimes," she giggled, cutting the tension.

"I have a question," I wanted to change the subject so I thought of the first thing I could think of.

"Shoot," she said going with the flow.

"Have you ever gotten lost in such a big house?" My question was sincere but she took it as a joke.

She laughed and I joined in, I guess it was a silly thing to ask. "No, but one time I was late for dinner because I went down the wrong corridor."

"Yeah, you have to be careful about those things." Talking to her was easier than I expected.

"So, now can I ask a question?" She said sitting up and leaning over me. I don't know why it made me uncomfortable but all I could think of was Annabelle. Even though I had abandoned her, I still had the hope of reuniting.

"Uh, sure." I held my breath.

"What is with you and that church? I admire you trying to fix it up but it seems to be an obsession." I avoided Crystal's look, I didn't want anything to be misconstrued by even the slightest of glances.

"Well, I just think that it is nice to give back to the community and since I am staying there I might as well put some work into it. Plus, people visit the church like Gareth...Gareth!" I sat up, knocking Crystal to the side. "Sorry," I apologized as she composed herself. "I didn't want to leave him alone for this long. We have to go back." I stood up and ran back to the horses. Crystal followed but she didn't seem too happy about it.

"I needed this," I admitted as I mounted the horse. "Maybe we can do it another time?"

"Yeah, maybe." Crystal smiled. "Race ya back?"

She took off towards the Heap. Spurring the horse I bolted after her. I understood something that I didn't even think of before. I am more in control than I think. I couldn't decide my own fate, but I could control how I act upon it.

We arrived back at the Heap, Crystal had beat me just by a hair. She was a very skilled rider and her ability and speed far outweighed my limited experience. "Better luck next time." She winked as she helped me get the two horses back into the stable.

We walked out of the stable and stood there in silence. "It's late, I should go," she said

"Yeah, I should get back to the church." I agreed.

"Right, the church. Listen Barnaby, like I said, don't let this consume you. You are a good guy, live a little." Crystal looked at me and softly smiled. It wasn't that I didn't want my life back, I just had a lot of people counting on me.

"Hey," I stopped her as she began to walk away. "I promise that I will give myself something to fight for, something that I want."

She smiled and rushed into my arms. "That's all I ask." We broke apart and looked at each other. Even though it was getting darker by the minute now, I could tell both of us were blushing.

Turning quickly she scurried away, hiding her face. Walking through the Heap at night was different than during the day. The bars were filled with drunks and the marketplace was closed, leaving the square in an eerie silence. Gusts of wind pushed me forward as I walked. The church was lit up from the inside, *Gareth must still be inside,* I thought. I felt guilty for leaving him in there. I hoped he wasn't too lonely.

Opening the door I felt a familiar but strange presence.

My guard immediately went up as I stepped inside the room. "Gareth?" I said with caution.

"Barnaby you are here, great!" I heard his voice from the front row of pews. He was with someone else, a man for whom I had mixed feelings for.

"Hello Barnaby," he said flatly.

"Hello Michael." I was happy to see him because I knew he was here to help, but I could do without his personality.

"Looks like you have been busy." He sounded snarky.

"I took a few hours for myself." I said knowing I wouldn't live this down anytime soon.

"We have a lot of work to do," he reminded me sternly. There was no arguing with him. He was always right and in his eyes, I wasn't allowed to act like a human anymore. I had to be able to keep up with him.

I rolled my eyes. "How are you doing, Gareth?" I asked completely ignoring Michael.

"Good. Michael and I have been talking. He is the angel from your story, isn't he? He is really nice." Gareth seemed very happy knowing Michael. I looked from Gareth to Michael. Was it just me who he hated?

"That's good. Maybe you should go get some rest. Come by tomorrow, okay?" I said to Gareth.

"Okay." He said standing up and walking over to the door. "Bye Michael, bye Barnaby." With that Gareth left.

Without so much as a moment Michael jumped on the

opportunity to point out something I had done wrong. "Have you any idea what risk you put yourself in?" He was beginning to badger me.

"I don't need this right now." I felt like a child saying this, but the truth of the matter was that Michael wasn't going to like me no matter what I did or said.

"We need to focus, the time for action is now." Michael shouted.

"I haven't been sitting around, I already recruited four people who are willing to fight for something you couldn't even handle yourself." I was walking on uneasy ground. Insulting Michael's ability to handle this situation was not my best move and I could tell instantly that I had hit a nerve.

Michael was quiet, like he was recalling a distant detail. Then out of nowhere he started to tell a story that hung in the room like fog in the night. "When they stormed the gates, I was at the right hand of God. The Old Man stopped me before I could aid the others. He said 'let the darkness come, this is light's ultimate test.' I didn't understand His reasoning and I argued with him to let me fight. But, He demanded I stay. I watched as hundreds of my brothers and sisters were cut down." He sighed. "Its not that I couldn't handle it, it was that I was asked to let it go."

"I am sorry, I didn't know." I lowered my voice.

"I know, go get some rest, tomorrow we will play catch-up and do what we need to do." Michael turned his back and faced the altar.

I didn't know what to say. I felt bad for Michael for once, I didn't know his side of the story and I judged him for being the way he was. However, trying to make anything more of the conversation was pointless, so I climbed the ladder to the bell tower and went to bed. If anything did come out of tonight's conversation it was this: I had peeled back a layer of Michael's past, and it revealed pain. Something I could relate to. Who knew I would have something in common with the Archangel?

— Chapter Sixteen —

Our Motley Crew

I woke from a rather restful sleep. I had almost forgotten what that felt like. I had to face Michael again. If we didn't come to terms and find common ground, how were we ever supposed to convince anyone else that we could lead them?

Wasting no time, I climbed down the ladder and went over what I wanted to say in my head. Michael was already standing in the room waiting for me. "Hey Michael, listen," I began, but he cut me off.

"Save it, I have something to say." Then through clenched teeth he uttered these words. "I apologize."

"Wait, what?" I was shocked, here I thought I was to blame because I was being selfish and not focusing on the cause.

Michael gave me a look which was a clear sign he wasn't going to say it again. "Well now that, that is out of the way, let's get the troops together." Michael walked towards the door.

"Who?" I was still confused from when he apologized.

"The people you recruited? Please tell me they are around here somewhere." Michael rolled his eyes and shook his head.

"Yes, of course." I opened the door to the church. "After you."

"This is going to be good." Michael muttered walking out.

"I don't really understand you." I said trying to keep up with Michael.

"Too bad, I am pretty cool once you get to know me." Michael laughed a little, which was a huge surprise.

"What has gotten into you?" I asked.

"What do you mean? I am fine." Michael did seem to have a hop in his step.

"You apologized to me. I know we haven't known each other for long, but that doesn't seem like you." He just came off as someone who was too hard-headed to admit they had made a mistake.

"You wouldn't understand." He brushed my question aside in a carefree manner.

"Try me." I pried.

"Fine, suit yourself. Everything is starting to take shape. War is beginning and I will have my revenge." This was pretty dark for an angel.

"Michael you shouldn't think like that." I never expected an angel to think this way. I thought they were peaceful and used words to resolve conflict.

"There is more to being an angel than the stereotype. This is very important to remember on your journey, Barnaby." Michael was clearly not an angelic stereotype. "Everyone is different, everyone has their own driven purpose."

"And yours?" I asked as we stopped at the steps of the manor.

"I was created on the basis of strength and courage. To lift up those who look to me. I charge into the darkness to bring forth light and I will put down nature's evil." Michael was truly serious now. "If I fail, may my wings be cut from my body and may I fall to earth." Michael carried himself with respect, for his title and his pride were both balanced upon his shoulders.

Michael knocked hard on the doors to the manor where Crystal lived. "I don't think anyone is home," I said after he tried knocking for a third time.

"Patience is a virtue." With that, Michael kicked the door in.

"What are you doing?" I yelled. Michael had no right to go kicking someone's door in randomly, angel or not.

"Shut up, something isn't right here." Michael curled his hand around the handle of his sword.

"You just kicked in their door, I think you are the one who isn't right here!" I couldn't believe what I had witnessed.

Michael drove his arm into my chest pinning me against the doorway. "I said shut up." He drew his blade and carefully stepped inside. Catching my breath I followed silently behind him. If Michael did sense something, then it was best to have him in front because I was unarmed.

The interior of the manor was enormous. It was even bigger than the Devil's home, but surprisingly simple compared to the exterior. "Hello? Crystal?" I said in a hushed tone although loud enough for my voice to echo up the main staircase.

Michael turned and looked sternly down at me. "You really can't keep quiet, can you?"

"Sorry." I stepped back, giving him room to do whatever he does. He was on high alert and when the angel of courage is wary of something, it is best to do what he says, when he says.

We walked up the stairs cautiously, trying not to make any noise. The manor's main staircase was marble, and came to a fork that led to the west and east wings.

"Should we split up?" I asked.

"No, it will be safer to stay together." Michael went down the west wing and I closely followed behind. We came to a closed wooden door. Murmured voices could be heard.

"That sounds like Crystal." I whispered.

"Let's see who she is talking to." Michael creaked open the door. Inside the bedroom were four people: Crystal, Gareth, an elderly gentleman, and a young man who looked out of sorts. He was disheveled, with long greasy hair, and his skin had a tinge of grey. The man had a shifty tic where he would dart his eyes around and blink very fast. His clothes were black and hung like loose rags over his slim figure.

"Hello there." Michael said with open arms.

"Hi Michael, this man is a bad man." Gareth pointed to the stranger.

"Michael?" The man said with confusion.

"Do you know him?" I asked.

"I know what he is." Michael said taking a step forward.

The man grabbed Crystal and held a knife to her neck. "Come any closer and she dies."

"That's a little extreme." Michael said laughing.

"That's my daughter, please don't test the man!" The elderly man must have been Crystal's father. He was short and pudgy with white hair. He reminded me a lot of Colonel Reynolds, actually.

"He isn't going to kill her." Michael took another step forward and the man pressed the blade closer to Crystals' neck she let out a small scream.

"Michael no!" I called, running forward and stopping him. "We can talk this out, can't we?" I suggested.

"Barnaby? I don't think you understand what is going on." Michael pointed out. "He is a demon, he came to spread death, and death there shall be." Michael lifted his sword. "Lets see what you're made of."

In a flash, the man tossed Crystal and her father aside as he morphed into the demonic beast. He looked like a terrible lizard that had long spikes sticking out of his back. A tail grew and his neck doubled in length. The man that was average in height was now a ten-foot monster. He didn't even look human anymore; he was more like a dragon, but without the wings.

"Get everyone out of here, he's mine." Michael and the beast faced off.

"Come on, let's go sweetheart." Crystal's father said, rushing her to the door.

"Come on Gareth." Crystal called, Gareth got up from his chair and scurried across the room.

"Good luck Michael!" he said as they left.

"You too, Barnaby," Michael didn't take his eyes off the demon.

"I'm staying, I have to get used to this sooner or later don't I? I can't leave you to fight every demon that comes our way." I walked over to the small dresser in the room and picked up a lamp, "I am sick of running from my problems. It is time to fight, not flee."

"You are going to fight me every step of the way, aren't you?" Michael moaned.

"Yep." I made the first move and ran for the demon. It let out a shriek and charged. When we made contact, it swept me off my feet and threw me across the room easily.

I rebounded just in time to witness Michael's fighting style. He charged at the demon like he was going for a jog in the park. Everything was cool, calm and collected when it came to the sweeping motion of his sword.

The lizard-like demon swung hard with its massive tail. Michael came crashing down and his sword flew from his hand and slid across the floor. Then with its jagged teeth, the demon bit down hard on Michael's arm. Blood started to pour from it. "Is that all you got?" He tried to shake the beast from his arm but it had a firm grip on him. "A little help here?" He grunted as he punched the demon in the face to no avail.

Running to the corner of the room, I picked up the sword and rushed to Michael's aid. "Hey," I yelled drawing the creature's attention. He let go of Michael and crawled towards me, baring its teeth and snarling.

Michael got up and pulled on the demon's tail, but he was kicked aside by its hind legs. For it was fixated on me, like it could see nothing else. "Barnaby run now, please!" The fact that Michael said please was warning enough. I eyed the door, the creature was blocking what would have been a clear path to the hallway. I would have to fight my way there.

Dodging the demon's bite I made a break for it. Unfortunately, I wasn't fast enough to avoid his tail and yet again I was whipped backwards onto my back. The room was spinning now. As the demon stood over me I did the only thing I could. Just as it was about to bite down, I drove the blade into its mouth. It let out a shriek and shook its head, trying to knock loose the blade lodged in its jaw.

During all of this Michael had regained his stance and came barreling for the demon. Grabbing hold of the beast's neck, he yanked the sword free.

"Don't make me ask again!" Michael scowled at me as he sliced into the arm of the demon, severing it.

I listened to him this time and raced down the hallway. Just as I heard the door slam behind me, I heard a loud crashing noise. Glancing over my shoulder I saw the demon hobbling towards me with blood spewing out of its missing limb. I screamed as I came to the stairs.

Crystal, her father and Gareth were all in the entrance of the manor. "Watch where you are going lad!" Crystal's father yelled as I split the group, running away from the demon that was hot on my heels. I made my way out of the manor, all the while thinking about the possible places in which I could hide. Would the church be a safe place? Could demons enter the house of the Lord?

I don't know why I did it; I should have just kept running, but for some reason I thought I was safe because everyone around me was going about their normal business. I stopped and turned around to look back at the manor. With a stone-crumbling explosion, the demon came rocketing out of the house of Lawless. It landed only feet from me and roared loudly into my face. "Uh, hi." I answered. The beast's left arm, or lack thereof, was dripping in blood. Any other animal would have bled out my now. However, it was unfazed and continued to look at me with hunger and lust.

A crowed formed, leaving the demon and I in some sort of arena-like stage. But I wasn't alone; to my surprise Nathan and Andrew joined my side.

"Well, this isn't what I pictured." Andrew said.

"It looks like a dinosaur." Nathan sounded more astonished than afraid.

In their company I felt like I had more of a fighting chance. Andrew had actually shown up to the scene with two throwing hatchets, but both Nathan and I were unarmed and that was not something I wanted to be.

The demon twitched and suddenly began turning back into a man. The three of us and the crowd held our breath. When the creature was gone, all that stood in its place was a smiling, crooked, grey-faced man. He was missing an arm but he didn't seem to mind. The bleeding had stopped and all that was left was an empty sleeve. "Hello Barnaby." He hissed.

"Who are you?" I asked.

The demon took a step forward. "A scout. A messenger to deliver this."

"What message?" I stepped forward and there was a small gasp in the crowd. Out of the corner of my eye I saw Kella. This could be the only time I would be able to get her attention, so I had to tell her indirectly what I needed to say in order to sway her join our cause.

The man took his time; he wanted to savor the moment. "Lennox calls." It was a simple message but the Devil sending scouts after me could only can mean that he was in the area and trying to track me down.

It was now time for me to send a message back to Lennox, a message that would also tell the crowed around me who exactly I was and what exactly I planned on doing.

"Thats all he said? Then tell him his. Barnaby calls, he calls for the good and the ones who hope." I looked around. I saw the faces of the women and the children and the men who would be killed by this crisis regardless of the outcome.

"Also tell this to your Devil. There will come a time, after I have gathered the angels and those who choose to follow, that I will find him on the battlefield of Judgment and I will kill him." With that I turned to Andrew and grabbed one of his hatchets. Turning back to the man I lunged for him.

He swiftly morphed back into the demonic creature and we met head on once more. This time I wasn't thrown back, I was putting up a fight. I cut into the demon's other arm, then its leg. I dodged what would have been a fatal bite and then I jumped over the whip of its tail.

An arrow flew through the air and struck the beast in the neck. It shrieked and the crowd scattered. The timing wasn't going to get any better, and the stupid idea I had bubbling up inside wasn't going to improve either, so I decided to go for it.

I ran for the creature and grabbed the arrow that was in its neck. Using it as leverage, I flipped myself onto its back as if to ride the beast. Yanking the arrow out, I drove it straight into the demon's skull. I was thrown off as the creature wobbled and groaned. Then it stopped and looked directly at me, baring its bloody teeth. I started to crawl backwards as it stepped forward. My bold move hadn't paid off.

Before the demon could take one more step, Michael jumped through the air and landed between the creature and me. He swung striking the demon's neck, slitting the beast's throat. The demon finally fell to the ground.

"That went well." I said walking over to Michael.

"Usually, it isn't this messy. You must be slowing me down," he criticized me every step of the way.

"Well, I think we make a good team." I tried to make light on the situation.

"Don't push it," he added, sheathing his sword.

Nathan and Andrew walked over to us. I could only imagine what could be going through their minds.

"What is their weakness?" Nathan asked. "Its arm was off and it didn't care."

"That's the trick, each one has a different weakness, just like you and me. But, all of them hate light and I'm not talking about the light from the sun, I am talking about pure light, created by God." Michael explained.

"You must be Michael." Nathan guessed.

"Yes, and you?"

"I am Nathan and this is Andrew, we have decided to join Barnaby on his quest." Nathan shook Michael's hand.

"Your skills?" Michael asked.

"What do you mean?" Nathan didn't expect this question.

"What are your skills? Are you a warrior? Why do you fight? Why do you exist?"

"Oh, well, I'm not much of a fighter, in fact I don't believe in it at all." This was news to me, how could Nathan get through this trip without going against this belief, especially after what he just witnessed, did he expect to not raise a hand? It was tough to accept for myself, but it's true; the road to hell is paved with good intentions and the road to heaven is paved with life's misguided discretions.

"I always knew that something or someone was out there looking down at us. I'd be damned if I gave up my opportunity to be a part of it all." Andrew's answer wasn't the first impression I wanted Michael to hear either.

"Let me get this straight, we have a pacifist and a daydream believer on our side." Michael turned to me. "Nice team you assembled here."

"We need them, you don't know them like I do." Standing up to Michael was second nature to me now. I felt like I had known him my entire life and we had always been like this.

"No, what we need is people like them." Michael pointed to a group of people standing only a few yards from us. They stood there looking at the dead demon. They were the only ones who had been brave enough to get close to the thing.

"Look Barnaby, it's Kella. She witnessed the whole thing. King and Destan are with her. This is our chance go talk to them." Nathan pushed me forward.

Trying to decide what to say, I walked up to the three of them. They were more and more intimidating with each step I took. "Hi." I said, coming to a halt right in front of the beast.

"Are you the one referred to as Barnaby?" the man named King asked. He was tall, muscular, and bald. He was dark skinned and his eyes were light brown, he held a spear. His clothing was handmade from cow hide. I knew from talking to Nathan that Destan, King's brother, is mute. In this situation, to convince King was to convince Destan.

"Yes?" I didn't know whether or not this would work in my favor.

"The Devil is after you?" He was curious.

"Yes." I wasn't going to lie to the man, he saw a demon in person specifically say to me that Lennox or rather the devil was calling for me.

"Were you serious about going after him?" The question was odd, like King was interested in my movement.

This looked like a good sign so I went with it, but I proceeded with caution. "I'm on a mission from God, whether you believe it or not. I was asked to gather the surviving angels and create a force to stand against the Devil and his army on Judgment day." There was silence and I jumped on the opportunity. "I need the help of anyone who wishes, to raise a free army." I looked right at Kella. "That is why I followed you that day. Nathan said you were the best around and I can't afford not to continue without you." I was cool in the beginning but now I didn't know if had said too much. The silence killed me.

Then King spoke. "There will be more of these things?" He asked.

"There will be thousands more and this isn't even the worst of it, this is just a scout." Warning them of the inevitable, whether they decided to join me or not, wasn't what I initially wanted to do; but if it works it works, and in these desperate times I did what I had to do.

"Sounds like you have a problem." Kella looked at the dead demon and shrugged.

"It is your problem too if I can't stop it." This wasn't so much of a threat as it was the truth.

Destan tugged at his brother's shirt. King looked at him and a silent conversation began between the two; with one nod a million things happened.

King looked back to me. "I don't like you, I find you clumsy and weak. You are a boy who claims to be a man, however, my brother has seen past everything you are not and sees worth in your cause. We will not follow you, but we will keep you from failing." Though King was insulting and showing no faith in our success, I was more than happy to set my feelings aside to have him join our team. These two were strong and able to hold their own. It didn't matter that Nathan wasn't a fighter, because we had gained two.

"I'm not going to die rotting away in this town if the world's ending. Unfortunately, you can count me in too. I'm going to hell in a hand basket anyway, so I might as well go down fighting." With Kella joining as well everything just clicked. I now had a complete team. I couldn't believe it.

Chapter Seventeen

The Footprints

"Are you all right my boy?" Mr. Lawless asked as he stood in the gaping hole where his door used to be.

"Yes sir, sorry about your door." I said as we walked up the stairs to the manor. Michael, Nathan, Andrew, Kella, Destan and King were all standing behind me.

"I am Frederick Lawless, Crystal's father and owner of the Heap. I want to thank you for fighting off that beast. I thought he was going to kill us." Mr. Lawless stretched out his hand and I shook it. "How can I ever repay you?"

"May I speak with Crystal?" I asked.

"Excuse me." Mr. Lawless' chest puffed out.

"He's fine Daddy, really now, come in, come in." Crystal said appearing through the hole.

Mr. Lawless composed himself. "Oh, where are my manners, come in."

"What was that thing?" Crystal said as she led us into a huge room with a long table that ran up its center. Between the chandeliers and the candles on the table, I would say there were over one thousand candles, in that one dining room. The walls had paintings of gardens. This was probably one of the more classier rooms of the estate.

"A demon." I answered.

"I didn't think they would look like that." She sounded nervous.

"You can still decide to step down. If you do, I won't think of you any differently." I didn't want to see her get hurt; I knew that she would if she came along.

She looked at me with a mixture of determination and confidence. "I made a promise to you and a promise to Gareth. I am coming and that's the end of it."

"I guess that settles it, then." I smiled.

"Going where?" Mr. Lawless asked from behind us. He didn't sound too happy.

Crystal looked from me to her father. "I am going with Barnaby and the others. There are more creatures like that out there and we have to stop them. Please understand." She sounded regretful.

"I forbid you from going!" He argued. "I almost lost you today and I will not, by any means, lose you again to those, those things!"

"Sir, she will be in good hands," I tried to convince him but I think I only made things worse.

He looked at me with dagger eyes. "You almost got yourself killed today, how are you supposed to protect her?"

"I will make sure she is safe." Michael cut in now, but even his size was not enough to convince Mr. Lawless.

"Nonsense, you are no better. I will have none of this—all of you please leave." He rushed us to the hole in the wall where the door of the manor used to be and we found ourselves standing outside before we knew it.

"One down, six to go. These demons won't know what hit them." Kella said sarcastically.

"What do we do now, Barnaby?" Nathan asked, leaving all eyes on me.

I turned to Michael. "The demon that showed up today caught both of us completely off guard."

"May I make a suggestion?" King asked.

"Absolutely." I responded immediately.

"Let us visit the armory. Then, we shall leave in the morning." Although I didn't want to leave the Heap just yet, I couldn't ignore the obstacles ahead any longer.

"Okay, sounds good." The group started walking towards the armory, "I will meet up with you guys later." Everyone looked at each other and shrugged, then left. I didn't have any interest of going to the armory; the only place I wanted to be right now was the church.

From the time I first stepped foot into the tiny church of God to the present, a world had changed. From a decrepit, rotting structure to a stable, fresh, sturdy sanctuary, the new purpose of this building was strangely significant to me. I walked inside and felt a presence, like I wasn't alone. Seeing that the chapel was empty I climbed the ladder to the bell tower. There was something unworldly in the atmosphere and I needed to find out what it was. Opening the trap door I saw it—or rather, I saw Him.

"Hello." God smiled.

"God?" He always surprised me.

"I was just in the neighborhood and I thought I'd stop by, you seem troubled." He was right…again.

"How did You know?" I grinned.

"I am good at reading people. Now come here and sit beside Me." I sat next to Him as He instructed, "I have a present for you." God said, taking out a wrapped gift.

"What is it?" I know from church teachings that we all have gifts that God gives us and that we should use them. However, I never heard of God actually physically handing someone a gift.

"Open it and see." He smiled as I ripped open the package. I really didn't believe what I saw, but it made complete sense to me. It was a sword.

The angelic weapon was more of a piece of art than anything. It was crude and weathered. The silver tinge had become dark due to wear and tear, the handle was wrapped in a thick worn leather that provided comfort to the user. The pommel had an engraving, two small wings with the cross of the trinity in the center. What was so striking about it was its character, the sword had a feeling of loyalty when I held it.

"Thank you, I don't know what to say."

"You have sacrificed so much it is time something was given to you." He smiled. "Now, I know I usually don't condone killing. However, in times of peril one must act without normality and take up the reigns." God stood up, laughed and walked over to the window. "Barnaby, we all give off an aura. It is our beacon to the spiritual universe. As you go forward, your aura will continue to grow, because what you pick up on the way will amplify the senses of the soul that communicates with everything around you."

God could see that I had absolutely no idea what He was talking about. "Basically, you will be able to tap into senses others have yet to feel. You won't exactly be an angel, but you also won't exactly be a man. You possess certain aspects that both angels and man cannot relate to. Until this process is through, not even I will know for certain what power might emerge."

"This just gets better and better doesn't it?" I could't believe it.

"Don't worry, I will be with you every step of the way, like I always have." He was calm as always.

"God?" Something else crossed my mind.

"Barnaby?" He raised an eye brow.

"Why do I feel as though I am connected to this building?" When I first entered the Heap and met Nathan, we made a deal that I would repair the church in exchange for room and board. Ever since then I felt like I was growing with each improvement I made to the structure. I felt like I wanted to work on it more and more as I progressed. I was proud of it and somehow I felt like it was changing something within me.

"Because you are connected to the church." God

continued. "As you gave life back into these old walls, something amazing happened. Did you notice that when you boarded the walls, you found Gareth sitting on the pew? How about when you and Gareth were painting?"

"Crystal showed up." I was beginning to understand it now. When I fixed different areas of the church, people began to come around. "But it only happened in those two instances, no one came when I fixed the other problems."

"I didn't want to make things too obvious." God smiled. "However, you still didn't finish the job, you know."

"I didn't?" I said scratching my head. I couldn't think of anything that was left undone.

With that God walked over to one of the crates in the bell tower and opened it. "Looking for something?" He said as He pulled out a cast iron handle for a door.

"That's it!" I said, realizing that one of the doors was missing a handle. It was the finishing touch to the restoration of the church.

"Go on." God winked, seeing that I was eager to finish what I had put so much work into.

I took the handle from Him and quickly made my way down the ladder. Then taking the hammer and nails from the pile of leftover supplies, I went outside and stood in front of the church.

Looking up, I saw God in the tower, watching with a sense of anticipation. I began to nail the handle carefully to the door of the church. It was finally done, after weeks of working. My mission in the Heap was over. I had recruited a team to accompany me on my journey and I had kept my promise to Nathan by restoring the church.

A commotion from the gate erupted. Turning around I saw a group of people assembled, some screaming, others just making noise. I heard one distinct voice shout out, "There are more of them!"

Instinctively, I took action. Suspecting another possible demon attack I ran back into the church and rushed up the ladder. The sword that God gave to me would be most useful against anything that isn't of Him.

God wasn't there anymore, which didn't surprise me. All that was left was the sword on the cot. I grabbed it and looked out the window to get a better look at what was going on.

"We aren't demons!" an annoyed voice shouted.

"Please, we come in peace." Another voice sparked something from my past.

"My name is Darius Crow, sergeant major of Gideon's Eastern Bounty State Trooper Corps, can anyone help us?" My heart almost stopped. Putting two and two together I realized the other voices belonged to Annabelle and the Preacher. How could they show up here at a time like this?

I was frozen. I had thought about Annabelle almost constantly since I left her and the Preacher in the cabin that night, only to wait for the moment when I would see her again. To answer to her, face to face now would be a nightmare. I stepped away from the window and sat on the cot dropping the sword onto the ground.

No pride, no dignity, nothing is what I felt. It was simply abandonment on my part, the shame of my past knocked on my door and I had no choice but to become a prisoner in my own home, my own body.

I stood up again. My legs shook and my stomach felt like it was being tossed up and down into the air. I crept to the window again to get another glance at Annabelle.

I looked out, scanning across the crowd. Then I found her, or rather she found me.

Annabelle squinted up at the tower and her mouth fell open, but that quickly turned into a scowl. She made a beeline for the church. I was done for as I heard the door slam underneath me. I debated on whether or not to just jump out of the window. The trap door flew open and Annabelle crawled through. We looked at each other in silence; there was a tear in her eye.

"How could you?" she demanded.

"I…." I didn't have an answer. I had done wrong in every way.

"Answer me, I deserve an answer!" Annabelle did deserve an answer, but I didn't have one to give her. "I said answer me!"

She pushed me backwards, causing both of us to fall onto the cot. We lay there motionless, her head on my chest as she cried. The girl who I thought couldn't be moved, was crying.

"Why did you leave us, why did you leave me?" Her muffled voice pulled at my heart strings; as if it wasn't enough that she was hurt by my absence, she took it personally.

"I wanted to protect you from what was coming for me." Even though this was the absolute truth, it didn't help.

"I could have been by your side through the worst. We started this together when they came for us in Gideon, what makes you think I wouldn't want to be with you until the end?" This got me; we had developed something by sharing these experiences. Once again, I had overlooked this in my attempt to prevent her from harm.

Enough was enough. I had to tell her how I felt. Maybe then, she would understand why I couldn't take her with me. It was not only the fact that I didn't want to see her hurt but if something happened to her because of something I did, then it would be impossible to press on. We sat up and she took a seat beside me. "I have to tell you something."

The trap door swung open and Nathan's head popped through. "Hello Barnaby— Sorry, did I come at a bad time?" He looked like his mind was somewhere else.

With a heavy sigh I came to realize that now might not be the best time to tell Annabelle how I felt. "No, it is okay. Did you need something?...Oh, this is Annabelle by the way." I said almost forgetting to introduce her.

Nathan looked at her with a half smile. "Hello Annabelle, lovely to meet you." Then he quickly looked back to me. "I need to talk to you about something. It is rather personal to me and I believe it relates to our current situation." He had caught my concern; he was a very easygoing guy and helped me through this process, if he needed my help in any way I would be there without question.

"Sure Nathan, just give me a minute, I'll meet you outside." Nathan nodded and when the trap door closed I looked at Annabelle. Our faces were close to one another and we were both looking into each other's eyes. "I hate to do this, but—" She stopped me.

"I understand, I'll be waiting here for you when you get back." She smiled as she wiped her eyes with her sleeve. She was beautiful, even with her hair askew and dirt on her face. She was the only thing I saw and the only thing I wanted to see.

I headed down the ladder and out the church doors into the cool dusk air. Nathan was standing there with a lantern. "Ready?" he said.

"Where are we going?" I asked.

"To my house." Nathan and I walked in silence. He was down about something, but what?

After walking down a dirt path that was lined on both sides with small wooden and dried mud brick huts we stopped at what could only be Nathan's home. It was very simple, there was one step that led up to a plain door with a lock on the knob. Nathan took the lantern and hung it on a hook that was next to the door. Then turned to me.

"Now, I know with everything going on this is the last thing you need to be bothered with."

I stopped Nathan right there, I owed him a lot, he couldn't bother me. "What is it?" I asked.

"All right…I have a brother, he is a bit different. I am all for helping you but I don't know what I am going to do with him when it comes time to actually **do** something." Nathan didn't mention his brother before, how different could he be?

"You can bring him with us if you want." I offered, however when I did, Nathan's face looked even more worried.

"What's wrong?" I asked.

Nathan looked at the ground and then to the door. "Why don't you just see for yourself."

Nathan went over to the door and unlocked it. Slipping the lock into his pocket, he opened the door and walked inside the very dark home.

I followed and immediately I felt a cold and terrible feeling.

"Barnaby, are you all right?" Michael asked as I heard his voice echo in my thought.

"Yes, I'm fine," I answered back. The fact that me and Michael were somehow communicating didn't come off as strange. I was beginning to think nothing would anymore.

"I feel that you are in the presence of a great evil," he warned.

"It's fine, I can handle it." I knew he was looking out

for me however I trusted Nathan.

"Who is that?" A strange and ominous voice swept across the tiny room, I couldn't see the person who spoke, but I didn't like his tone.

"Duncan, this is my friend Barnaby." Nathan's voice was shaky.

"A friend? No friend of yours is a friend of mine. Tell him to leave." Duncan demanded in a harsh belittling bark.

"Tell me yourself." I spat back taking a stand for both of us.

In the dark I saw Nathan flash a smile at me, like I had done him a great favor.

Duncan let out a low haunting laugh. "Fine have it your way, take a seat, Barnaby." He hissed.

I sat down in a small squeaky chair. "Tell me about yourself," I said, facing the dark corner where the voice resonated from. I engaged Duncan in conversation right away; I wanted to keep him talking.

"What is there to say? I am locked up in this shit for a shack and I barely see the light of day. My idiot brother over here claims that he keeps me here for my own good, but I know the reason. I want a life that is more than this."

"What kind of life do you want then?" What was the driving force of Duncan Porter?

"I'm waiting" Duncan left this as open as he could.

"For what? I played along.

Duncan leaned out from the dark corner of the room, what appeared was a pale faced, sickly looking man. He had bloodshot eyes and red shaggy hair; his crude and curled smile left a snickering charm that disturbed me. "What am I waiting for, you ask? The Judgment of course, for when the Judgment comes the ones who have been condemned will rise and fight good's glorified swine, a new regime will be formed, and the true God will forever make us thrive." He leaned back disappearing into the darkness. "Now leave, you are boring me." Nathan and I both stood up without saying a word and began walking out. "Oh and Barnaby," Duncan taunted. "See you on the front lines."

Nathan closed the door and locked it, he turned and looked at me. "What do you think?" he said, looking rather embarrassed.

"He seems nice." I didn't know what to say, I didn't see this coming. I thought demons and the devil were the only things that faced us, but sympathizers for the devil? This was going to be a war of choice.

"I don't know if I can take up arms against my own brother." Everything Nathan was feeling was understandable; he didn't have to fight.

First we lost Crystal and now Nathan. The dream team I thought I had assembled was coming under fire before it even entered the battle.

"I'm sorry..." Nathan looked at the ground, hiding his face.

Nathan and I parted as friends, and still the closest of allies. As I walked back to the church I wondered about other people's problems. I had been so focused on mine that I neglected to think that others found themselves in the same boat. We were all riding the rough currents of life in a leaky lifeboat.

"Hello, Preacher. It is late, isn't it?" The Preacher was taking a stroll past the church when I ran into him.

"I can say the same to you." He chuckled. "I am just here gazing at the stars and the moon, searching the cosmos for an answer, just like the rest of us."

I joined him and looked up at the night's wonderment. "With all respect Preacher, don't you look to God for the answers?"

"God is everywhere and everything. He is the stars and the clouds, the rain and the drought, He is the tiniest of pebbles in a quarry to the mightiest oak in the forest. There cannot be one way of communicating with Him if He communicates with me in so many different ways. What would you like to say to God?" He asked continuing to look up at the sky. I looked up as well, my eyes darted from the moon to the stars.

"What will you take from me?" I let out.

"What an odd question." The Preacher acknowledged.

"Everything." The voice that answered dissipated with the wind, the Preacher didn't seem to hear it though.

I knew God was speaking to me at this moment. "Can I

prevent walking away with a life worse than death?" I felt connected, like I was plugged in to a circuit board waiting for a response from the other end of the line.

The Preacher was concerned now. "What is bothering you?"

"Preacher, a storm is coming and I am ground zero." The Preacher was a man of faith and God. Above all, he knew I needed someone right now.

"Come, sit with me." We sat at the church steps, "now, tell me everything."

So, I did. I told my story for what felt like the hundredth time. An hour must have passed and at the end, the Preacher just closed his eyes and shook his head. "That pretty much sums it up." I said looking at my feet.

"The final reckoning will come, follow with trust my second born son." The Preacher finally said.

"Yeah, I am starting to think I know what that means now." I admitted. "The thing is though, I have to not only find these angels but complete these tasks that will test me in ways which man has never been tested before."

The preacher leaned into me. "If you would have me, I shall do my best to aid you."

"Of course", I responded. The Preacher would be an asset that I certainly needed; everyone was, in my eyes. "I have to warn you though, I don't have much of a plan."

"None of us do," the Preacher joked.

We sat there in silence as we both looked up to the stars.

"Preacher, what do you think defines a man?" My question must have sounded totally out of the blue. But the truth remained; it would take the strongest qualities man possessed to pull this off and I needed to know if I measured up.

Without skipping so much as a beat the Preacher chimed in with his answer. "You want to know what makes a man? What his adversaries say about him when they are standing over his grave."

"That's it?" I asked thinking there was more to it.

"What else is there for me to say? There isn't a clear answer. Some people know who they are the minute they come into this world, others only know who they are when they see who attends their funeral. Barnaby, never feel that you'll only be measured by opinions from those you meet in life. Seek only the judgment from God. For He is the one in which opinion truly matters." This was becoming truer and truer as the days passed.

"How do you see me? I mean, you must have an opinion." I wondered where the Preacher stood in all this.

"I see you as what you are, a man being pulled in different directions, neither knowing which to satisfy first nor which is the right path to take. I just don't want to be there when you are finally pulled apart." The Preacher stood up.

"At least you're honest, and since we are being honest may I say something that's been troubling me?" I was still sitting.

"Yes of course."

"How is it that I feel so alone when I know God is there?"

The Preacher took some time crafting his reply "Barnaby, have you ever heard the story of the footprints?"

"No." How could footprints help me, I wondered.

"It goes something like this: **One night I dreamed a dream. As I was walking along the beach with my Lord. Across the dark sky flashed scenes from my life. For each scene, I noticed two sets of footprints in the sand, one belonging to me and one to my Lord. After the last scene of my life flashed before me, I looked back at the footprints in the sand. I noticed that at many times along the path of my life, especially at the very lowest and saddest times, there was only one set of footprints.**

This really troubled me, so I asked the Lord about it. "Lord, you said once I decided to follow you, you'd walk with me all the way. But I noticed that during the saddest and most troublesome times of my life, there was only one set of footprints. I don't understand why, when I needed You the most, You would leave me."

He whispered, "My precious child, I love you and will never leave you, during your trials and testings. When you saw only one set of footprints, it was then that I carried you."

The Preacher let the story float in the air for a moment. "You see, even though you are aware of God, it doesn't mean you don't question his presence throughout your life. There will be times where even now you feel as though God has abandoned you. However, during these times He is actually the closest to us. Just like in the story, God will always walk beside us. He will always carry us when taking another step seems impossible." The wind brushed past and the leaves shook on the trees. "I must go now. Good night, Barnaby."

"Good night, Preacher." I said thinking of the story as it applied to my life.

When I returned to the bell tower, Annabelle was fast asleep. I was happy to see she was resting. I had a feeling that tomorrow everything would change, but what kept me up for the rest of the night was the question of whether or not it was for the better or for the worse.

Chapter Eighteen

The Death of a King

The next morning there wasn't a cloud in the sky. It was one of those days where everything felt brand new. I was up before Annabelle, so I decided to go for a walk. Climbing down the ladder, I felt the presence of someone behind me. It was Darius.

"Oh, hello." He was the last person I expected to see. Seeing him at the gate yesterday confirmed he was alive, but at the same time I felt distant from him. I felt as though we drifted apart and all that remained was an unpleasant silence.

"If there was anything left of the Corps, I would strip you of what little rank you possessed," he said sternly.

"I can explain." I knew Darius wouldn't care what I had to say, and why should he? I was a trooper under his command and I had failed him.

"I don't want to hear it. You abandoned your post and fled without the order of retreat. You are a deserter, but none of that is important; you ran away from your friends do you understand that? Have you no honor?" Darius cut deep.

"No, I don't." I whispered lowering my head.

"At least you are man enough to come to terms with that." He walked from the altar toward me in a very dignified manner, with or without uniform. He was what this cause needed as its leader, not I.

"Darius, I am sorry." Someone who I looked up to was kicking me while I was down and there was nothing I could do about it.

"Apologizing is just a coward's way of trying to cover up something he didn't get away with." With that, Darius walked over to the doors of the church. "And another thing," he growled as he opened one of the doors. "If you are to lead at least one man into battle, lead from the front so your words may comfort those who are about to welcome death." I heard the door close and that was that, the reunion was over.

"You okay, Barnaby?" I turned and saw that Annabelle had been standing behind me.

"Yeah I am okay," I said even though I felt my eyes watering up a bit.

Annabelle gave me a hug. The little things were the only things now. I would have to accept that friends would come and go on this trip, but as long as she was with me everything would be all right. Annabelle backed off and once again we found ourselves looking into each other's eyes. She looked at my lips and bit her's softy, then she leaned in and...

The church shook, causing us to break apart. "Please tell me you felt that." I had a sinking feeling in my stomach and I knew the day had taken a turn for the worse.

"What do you think it could be?" Annabelle asked as she went over to the door and opened it. "Uh, Barnaby the Heap is burning." Her face went from worried to blank shock.

Lennox must be here. "Stay here," I shouted. Climbing the ladder, the smell of smoke and the sound of people screaming circled around me. As I took up my sword, I looked out the window of the bell tower. Just as I had predicted, Lennox, Vladimir, Naomi, Marx and Abigail were cutting through the town, setting it ablaze with no one to stop them.

One of the fire balls smashed into the church and smoke surrounded me in seconds. I was blown backwards as half the bell tower collapsed. I had no time; without wasting a breath I snatched up my pack that contained Elek and the horn. I slid down the ladder. Annabelle grabbed me and we both dashed through the doors just in time, for the entire church collapsed in on itself at that moment.

"All that work, just for it to go up in flames?" I was devastated that the church didn't survive. It had been my home, a place where I had grown so much.

"We have to go." Annabelle yelled, tugging on my shirt. Getting up we made our way through the smoke-filled air until we came to the manor. It was the only place where people could take refuge and a deep breath.

Immediately, I met with the others who were assembled at the steps of the manor. They were ready to fight—even the preacher had a weapon—but Nathan was not there. Michael looked at me and both he and I had a mutual understanding to put our differences aside at a time like this.

"All right, this is the first test, guys. Survive this and we will be able to pull through the rest." I didn't know how to inspire anyone with a fancy battle speech or anything that would be considered a rally, but I gave it my best.

"That wasn't very good." Kella instantly shot my attempt down.

"Get through today and I promise I'll get better at this kind of thing." I said, trying to shut her up.

"Works for me," she said, smirking.

"What is going on here?" Mr. Lawless came running out of his home. "What has happened?"

"The creatures I warned you about, they are back, Daddy." Crystal appeared from behind her father.

"You!" He pointed directly at me. "You brought them here and you have destroyed everything!"

"Sir, they wish to consume everything. They won't stop at me." It was no use, he was hysterical.

"I would have done anything they said to keep my family and people safe." He yelled, "and you had to go and destroy that."

"What, Daddy?" Crystal stepped back from her father with a look of confusion and disgust.

"Sweetheart, I would have done anything to save you from this." Mr. Lawless tried to embrace his daughter but she backed further away.

"Even if that means standing on the sidelines while everything and everyone is stepped over?" She demanded an answer with tears in her eyes.

"Yes." Even though he wouldn't think twice about doing just that, he was ashamed of how his daughter saw him now. But I didn't blame Mr. Lawless, he was just a father doing his job.

"Hello, Barnaby." The coldest shiver I had ever felt shot up my spine as Lennox called my name over the crowd. I turned slowly to see him standing there with a squadron of demons behind him. "How have you been?" he asked, smiling at me.

I walked down the stairs and stepped in front of the crowd. If Lennox was going to make a move for my life I wouldn't want anyone in the crossfire. "Fine. I can't say that it's nice to see you again, but here you are."

Lennox chuckled. "Indeed, well since I am here, how about you and I have a little chat."

"Sure." I wasn't sure where this was going.

"Let's make a deal," Lennox began.

"I was taught not to make deals with the devil." I cut him off.

"We can do this the easy way or the hard way. Come with me and they live, or don't, and they die." Lennox pointed his sword at the crowd, who inched back. I wasn't going to let the innocent die if I had a choice, and Lennox knew this about me.

There was a silence from both the crowd and the demons, all eager to hear my answer.

"Wait!" A man's voice called out from the manor, it sounded a lot like Darius. I turned and watched as Darius walked over to the Devil's side. "Got room for one more?" he asked.

Lennox looked at him for a moment, then his smile widened. "Sure, we need to replace Cain anyway," he joked.

"Darius?" I couldn't believe what I was witnessing.

"Don't start with me Barnaby, I am jumping off this ship before you take us all down with you." Darius was still very angry with me and now I was angry at him. The friendship we once had was now nothing but ashes.

Lennox glanced at both Darius and I who by now had drawn our swords against each other. "You two are friends? I see the plot has thickened," he chuckled.

"For God's sake son, I have made my fair share of mistakes but never have I sunk so far." Mr. Lawless started to yell at Darius.

"Shut it, old man. You just admitted that you would sell the world to the highest bidder so you and your daughter could continue to live in luxury." Darius was right, but it was the reasoning behind what the two men did that set them apart. One wanted to protect his daughter's future and the other just jumped ship to save his skin.

Mr. Lawless walked towards Darius and from his vest he drew a small golden dagger with red accents. "Stop!" I yelled, but it was too late. Darius drove his blade into Mr. Lawless' gut, he fell to the ground everyone remained silent, except for Lennox.

"Well, well, this has been quite the interesting day so far, hasn't it?" Lennox patted Darius on the back, "you'll fit right in."

Crystal ran to the body of her dying father. "Daddy, Daddy!"

"I'm sorry, I just wanted to protect you," he said as he kissed her forehead.

"I know Daddy, I know, please I know. Come back, I forgive you, please." There was nothing that could be done. She buried her face between his neck and shoulder and cried.

I couldn't hold back my anger. I lunged for Darius and he for me; we met and the clashing of our blades rang out against the walls of the Heap. I had never fought with such ease before. Each movement of the blade was smooth and in alignment with the next.

But, it was not enough. As I went around for another swing, Darius faked right and cut into my leg, I fell to my knee but I wasn't going to give up—this was for Mr. Lawless and Crystal. Without wasting time the others jumped in to save me. But as they did, the demons stormed in creating an air of chaos and confusion. Taking advantage of the commotion I got up and faced Darius once more. How could he do this? He made sure that good always triumphed over evil, and now he embraces evil as if it were his brother.

"You know you're going to have to die now," Darius taunted me.

"Not before you." I lunged back and swung as hard as I could. We locked blades again and found ourselves in a fast-paced duel to the death. This time however, I landed a hit, right as

Darius was moving in for what would be a fatal blow. I slashed for his face, striking him in the cheek and eye. He screamed and covered the wound with one hand. He swung violently and randomly, blinded in one eye from his own blood.

I saw this as my only chance. I took Elek out of my pack and set him on the ground. "Elek, now!"

The ground shook and Elek morphed into the ancient protector. His roar made everyone on the battle field stop and stare as he shook the ground as he stomped and flashed his fangs. He towered over the demons.

"Elek," I called, "protect the others." Elek quickly began to attack the surrounding demons. One by one, he tore each of them apart. I needed to stay focused, my fight was with Lennox and Darius. But first, I needed to find Annabelle.

"Annabelle!" I called. "Annabelle!"

"Over here!" She called as she drove a spear into a demon's chest.

Limping over to her I grabbed her by the shoulders. "I have to tell you something." I said.

"Can't it wait?" she asked.

"No, not really." It was now or never. "Considering we are probably going to die today."

"Well, all right then" she said. "Hold on." She moved me out of the way and unsheathed the sword she had on her hip. She confronted a demon and swiftly cut a X into its chest. "What did you want to say?" She asked me.

"I love you," I finally said it.

"It's about time." She smiled. Without warning she wrapped her arms around me and kissed me. "I can read you like a book. Now let's live today so we can have a life together tomorrow."

"Whatever you say." My cheeks were on fire and suddenly the pain from my wounds vanished.

The fighting continued as more demons poured into the Heap. Amazingly, we were holding our own.

"Enough!" Lennox shouted. The survivors stopped.

He cleared his throat and composed himself. "You have all fought gallantly, but we can all agree that this is not a game, someone has to die and as you can see I have come more prepared." More demons came into the Heap. Lennox pointed at me. "You have a choice. Surrender and I will forgive your lapse in judgment, or die a fool's death and be forgotten to time." Lennox reckoned himself to be better than God.

"I stand as a man, a man who stands by his God and his friends." I was not backing down especially now, blood had been spilt.

"Would a God as great as you say let this happen to His people?" The Devil walked over to a dead body and pulled a sword out of its side. "Do you think your God is any less violent and any more holy than you and me? Face the facts, Barnaby. He is what makes men hate each other, He sits on the tops of tanks in war, He calls for the heads of power and drives tyranny that fuels itself with the enslavement of its own people. When will He answer your prayers? When will He come and take responsibility for His mistakes?"

"Now." No one had noticed the man until now, but once He removed his hood and revealed His identity I knew who it was. God.

The Devil looked like he had struck gold. "Finally, You have come out of hiding." Lennox signaled for two demons to restrain Him. "Too bad You will be rewarded with death because of it."

"No!" I said running over to Him, only to be stopped.

"Don't worry Barnaby, you will soon suffer the same fate as He." Lennox gestured for two more demons and soon I was restrained as well. "You should have just taken me up on my offer. You would be standing beside your friend now, on the side of victory."

"Our fight isn't over." I struggled to break free from the hold of the demons.

"You will die a fool then." Lennox looked to his army. "Take both of them with us, kill the others.

"Elek!" I shouted. "I'll be fine, protect them!"

Elek responded with a mighty roar and began to round up Crystal, King, Annabelle, Kella, and the Preacher. Unfortunately, he was not fast enough and the demons snatched up Destan, and Gareth in the commotion.

The Devil walked to the entrance and turned around.

"What was once a haven for those who lived here will now turn to ash, in fire it will bathe and its scorned walls will cover its fortuned past. I hope the revolution was worth the pain, because now your deaths are in vain." A fire ball formed in his hand and blew apart the manor; it burst into a blaze and quickly spread to the remaining buildings. He laughed and left the Heap to crumble in on itself, with Annabelle and the others all trapped inside. I yelled but nothing could be done. I was in the hands of the Devil, something that I swore wouldn't happen again.

Outside the Heap we were loaded into caged carts, two to each one. I was thrown into one with Destan, they were small and felt like they were about to fall apart with each turn of the wheel. Destan and I sat silently as we moved slowly down the hill.

"Wait up!" A faint voice stretched from the Heap; the caravan didn't stop. The faint voice called again and we kept pressing on.

A skeleton-like man ran past the cart; his red hair and pale skin made him stick out like a sore thumb.

"Devil. You there." He commanded.

Lennox ignored him and continued to walk along side the carts.

"Hey, didn't you hear me?" Duncan called.

The Devil turned and faced Duncan; he looked revolted by his presence. "Who are you?"

"Pleased to meet you, I am Duncan Porter. I was quite impressed with what you have to say and decided that you and I can be of some use to each other." Duncan extended his hand.

The Devil spit at Duncan's feet and turned his back on him.

"Didn't you hear me?" Duncan persisted.

"I heard you, now if you like your head leave my side. You may find a place in the ranks but remain there, for I have no use for you." Lennox dismissed him without hesitation. "But—" Lennox unsheathed his sword and put it to Duncan's neck.

"First rule, do as I say. Second rule, do as I say and if you must refer to the third rule then you are already dead, understood?" Lennox scowled.

"Understood." Duncan held his breath and slowly filed into the lines of demons, disappearing amongst the ranks.

"Where are we going?" I yelled to Lennox.

He didn't look at me, he just kept walking. "To your crucifixion," he announced.

— Chapter Nineteen —

From the Ashes we Fight

I woke up in a cell. It was cold and the sun was just rising. It had been days since we were taken and my body ached. My clothes were in rags and my vision was blurred. At this rate the conditions would do us in before what was in store.

The others weren't handling any of this any better. Destan was sitting in the corner staring at the floor and Gareth was rocking back and forth. God was being held somewhere else, His status unknown. I had the feeling that comes with failure, the need to dwell on things that are meant to be forgotten, the things that would drive men mad because of their intricate, minuscule details.

I thought about my brother Marshall, I thought about my father and my mother and the decay in which they lived in for months. I thought about the cold night, the night I met Edmund and the bread he gave me. I thought about the train ride and the moment I received Elek from Neo. I thought about the first time I looked into Annabelle's eyes and felt happy again.

The list went on and on. The first time I killed a man, the first meal I had with the Devil, the first conversation I had with God, everything was a first this past year. With everything new came the fear of losing everything old—old being the feeling of normalcy, of just talking with someone about something other than angels and demons or death and life. I craved real, human feelings, like when Annabelle and I kissed.

Vladimir stepped inside the old EBS Trooper jail house that we were being held in, accompanied by four demons all holding weapons at their sides. "All right," Vladimir approached the cell and opened it with a clanky old key, "come on."

The demons entered the cell and grabbed hold of us, forcing us up and out. They dragged us outside and down the road toward the center of the town. Struggling to stand, my legs scraped against the ground, so much so that I drew quite a bit of blood. The town surrounding the hill was completely destroyed, crumbled buildings were now mounds of debris that were covered in a thick fog and an eerie silence.

We reached the bottom of the hill and were forced onto our knees. I looked up to the crest of the hill where three crosses laid. Lennox wasn't kidding when he said crucifixion. I closed my eyes and my head dropped, "Come on, find a way out of this. Let faith overcome," I muttered under my breath. "Your fight can only be measured by the amount of times you get back up." I tried to pump myself up. I knew I could get through this, I had done it before.

Watching the hill I saw Lennox, Naomi, and Abigail take position in front of the Crosses, accompanied by Darius. When I saw him my stomach flipped. To think I had once called him a friend. Demons began to fill in around them, waiting for the ceremony to start. It would all be over soon.

"Lets go." Vladimir said. The three of us were pushed

forward and up the hill. We stood to the side waiting to be killed. The wind changed and the day went suddenly from clear to windy and cloudy. On the other side of the crowd stood God. He was guarded closely by Marx and ten other demons. He looked very gloomy, yet a sense of peace coated his face.

Lennox spoke. "We have come a long way. As many of you know this started many eons ago. With a group of cast-aside angels who dreamed of a better life, who planned to defy their God for one important purpose, to be given the will to be the masters of their own domain. The war that ensued for a millennia claimed many and tore apart the kingdom that was so mighty and bright. Its outcome, you ask? The exile of all those who raised up arms against the Heavenly Father, for He could do no wrong." Lennox laughed. "At first we failed to conquer what was all but ours, but through patience and preparation we have fought our way back to the top and we have finally and justly toppled the ones who kept that fortune to themselves." The Devil basked in the cheer from the crowd, then continued. "It is not enough just to take Heaven in order to claim victory. No, we must kill God Himself to sit in His chair, thus ushering in a new king, a powerful and fair king to rule the kingdom of creation. I feel that it is time for this change, don't you?" The crowd of demons erupted with cheer again. "Now then, to take out the old and bring forth the new. And so, it begins!"

Marx and the demons pushed God forward towards the center cross. Reaching the structure they took rope and laid God down upon it. They began to tie him up tightly, from his arms to his feet. The sky churned with heavy clouds; light barely managed to break through the thickness of the swirling winds and the air became darker and darker. The cross was then lifted into the air until it stood straight up and down, towering over the people. A slight rumble could be heard, something was happening.

"I will give You, what You never gave me before I was cast into the depths of Hell. A final thought." Lennox was loving every second of this torture.

Still calm and collected, God looked into Lennox's eyes with deep emotion as the rumbling of thunder grew louder and louder. "I believe there is good in you. Luckily, someone else does too." God then turned to me and gave me a look that a proud father would give to his son.

The thunder crackled right over our heads and a massive lighting bolt ripped through the air, striking the tip of the cross where God hung. It immediately splintered and came crashing down in a burning heap.

"No!" I screamed as the rain fell down hard and fast. The demons celebrated with tremendous cheering, after all they had done their job. The Devil however had a look of mixed emotion, a cocktail of triumph, guilt, and rage.

To be the Devil is not only to be hated but to also live a misunderstood life. This is a simple observation, but the fact was that before His death, God told the Devil He knew that there was good in him—something the Devil had been wanting to hear for ages. He had just killed the one Being who believed that fact. I remembered from our conversations that the Devil was bothered by the notion that everyone was always rooting for the other guy. It was clear now that the other guy had been rooting for the Devil all along.

Driven by the hype, Lennox silenced the crowed. "Your patience has been well appreciated and it will be well rewarded, but bear with me for one more moment. We will soon forever bask together in the spoils and riches of power and wealth. Bring forward Barnaby!" Lennox shouted.

I didn't resist, how could I? I was outnumbered a hundred to one. Without God, I questioned if hope was even still there. The rain picked up and the crackling of thunder and flashes of lighting seemed to double. The wind swept up debris that was scattered across the ground. I caught a worried glimpse between Naomi and Abigail. There came a point where I could barely hear myself think amid the noise of the wind and rain. Nonetheless I was brought up and laid upon the cross. Demons began to tie my arms and legs down.

"Hello, friend." Darius walked up and looked down at me. His face expressionless.

"I hope you understand that what you're doing is wrong." I spat back.

"We obviously have different priorities when it comes to right and wrong." He said with his nose in the air. I hated the fact that he thought he was better than me, after everything that had happened he still chose this path. Although, war does bring that out in people. War forces us to choose a side.

"I just have one thing to say to you." I said as the demons finished tying my feet.

"What would that be?" He asked.

"I didn't think you would have taken this much pleasure in killing me." The demons began to hoist the cross off of the ground. As it fell into place I felt the sting of the rain and winds. However, I would not release eye contact with Darius. If this was the last time he saw me alive, I wanted him to remember that I looked into his eyes with disgust and disappointment until my last moment on this earth.

Waiting helplessly for my time to end. Darius shook his head and turned his back on me.

"Hey!" I yelled over the wind. "Where are you going? Look at me! Look at what you've done!" I was furious. He was a coward for not witnessing firsthand what his betrayal had achieved. He had called me a coward for abandoning Annabelle, now he did the same to me? Nothing was adding up.

Try as I might I could not get Darius to turn his back. I was already dead to him. I looked out over the crowd, over Lennox, over the demons, over the town that was destroyed in the wake of some new kingdom, a kingdom filled with darkness and suffering. I looked to Gareth and Destan who stood restrained at the bottom of the hill. Looking up at me, their faces showed certainty of death. It reminded me of the angels and how they would be waiting with high hopes to be found, only to be met with the same cold fate that God just endured. Finally, I thought of Annabelle's soft face, and her smile.

I couldn't tell if it was rain or the tears that were cascading down my face, but at that moment I made a promise to myself. A promise that when I died and I got to where ever I was going, that I would do everything in my power to look after those whom I had let down. If I couldn't protect them in this life, then maybe in the next I could do some good.

I was practically hysterical now waiting for it to be over. "This has been an interesting sequence of events." I joked to myself. It was all over before it began, one small rebellion at the Heap's gates was all that could be said about the Devil's rise to power.

Maybe I spoke too soon, or maybe in the universe things are meant to happen in funny ways to keep us on our feet, but at that moment I felt a hand lift my chin up. Nothing was there causing the sensation, but I felt a slight nudge that made me hold my head high, high enough to look towards the horizon.

A cloaked figure stood at the base of the hill near the rubble of a building. He stood motionless and I barely noticed him. I would have missed him entirely if I hadn't felt myself being directed towards him.

Who was this man? Was he one of the surviving locals watching the festivities? It couldn't be God, could it? No, I had just watched Him die.

The answer came to me in one brief moment by flashback. **"Don't worry I've been assigned to guide you, however God will leave you in charge....God will leave you in charge...God will leave you."** The man was Michael, he had been assigned to me by God, a God who had left me in charge.

At that moment the figure removed the hood of the cloak from his head. Slowly, one by one, the demons turned around. All attention was on Michael now, but he didn't mind. Lennox turned and clapped. "Well, well." The storm continued to grow; the last place I wanted to be was on top of anything in a storm like this. "Brothers! Today is a day for killing Gods and angels! Rip his wings off, then take him to the cross!" The demons' cries of war shook the ground as they came charging down the hill towards Michael, who simply waited for them.

Just as the demons reached Michael he removed the cloak entirely, exposing two golden swords. Unsheathing them he began to slice his way through the crowed with agility and precision.

The Devil and his immediate followers showed anger, fear and confusion as they watched Michael slice through their forces with ease. It didn't take long for them to realize that they might suffer the same fate as their foot soldiers if they stuck around any longer.

"Can we leave?" I heard Abigail shout.

"We have won already, let us not risk ourselves for the irrelevant." Naomi added.

Lennox turned to me. "Goodbye Barnaby, I could have

hoped for a more worthy adversary." With that they left through a crumbling house.

As Michael fought off the demons, I felt the cross lower to the ground. Gareth and Destan began to untie my hands and feet. We were going to get out of this alive.

"It's okay, it's over now." Gareth said, comforting me. I wished he was right, but I knew the road ahead of us was long and filled with trials. Although, it was Gareth, and I couldn't help but flash a smile at his innocent optimism.

The three of us observed Michael's skill. It surpassed anything that the demons could match, they were so quickly cut down. Those lucky enough to escape scurried away like frightened children. Michael sheathed his swords. "Well, there you have it," he said, looking around at all the motionless bodies. "Now come on, let's go."

"There is nowhere to go. The Haven is destroyed and I have no idea where we are." I looked around.

"My job is just to protect you. You're the one who has to carry this out," Michael reprimanded. "We have to press on with the mission."

"I know, I know. Just let me think." I had no idea where we were.

"I know where we are." Gareth spoke up.

"You do?" We all turned to him.

"Yeah, Crystal and I used to pass through here on our way to Phoenix, we would go shopping for some pretty neat things."

He exclaimed. "We are about three days away, come on, follow me!" Gareth started to walk down the road.

"Perfect, we can get some supplies and see if we can contact the others." I said, following Gareth.

For the next hour or so we walked down the road that would eventually bring us to Phoenix. It gave me time to gather my emotions. I had survived of course, but at what cost? God was gone.

Suddenly, we stopped at the mouth of a tunnel. "What's the matter Michael?" Gareth asked.

"Someone is there," he peered into the tunnel, inching forward. Without warning Michael stopped and lowered his sword. "Really? Come on!" Michael looked up into the sky. "You know, I could have handled taking care of the kid on my own." Michael sheathed his sword and turned around. "Listen Barnaby, just give me the word and I'll send this guy packing."

"Send who packing?" Why didn't Michael want whoever it was around?

Turning back Michael confronted the man. "We don't need your help, we have everything under control. If you were here a couple minutes ago you could see that I am capable of dealing with it."

"Michael, who is it?" I asked stepping forward.

"Don't worry about it kid," he said, dismissing me.

Don't worry about it? I had to worry about everything at this point. Who was it and why was Michael acting so weird?

I nudged Michael aside. "Who are you?" I asked.

Out from the tunnel came a man, tanned, with long brown hair and eyes. His beard was shaggy just like his clothing. His hands were wrapped with white cloth and his smile was welcoming.

"Who are you?" I asked again as the man stepped more into the light.

"Hello, Barnaby. My name is Jesus."

EPILOGUE

The loud echo of slow moving footsteps made their way down a path of white marble. In the wake of each step was a mark of charred, burnt ground. Eyes fixed ahead to the prize that was all too sweet. The sound of nothing, in the purest form, deafened and suffocated the endless space. Gradually ascending pillars surrounded a single chair that was centered on top of a raised circular platform. It was the target. A mixture of golden and green vines hung from each pillar like hair on a child. One by one the footsteps made their anxious way forward, all the while leaving a trace of wilt and gloom. Plants that once bore their colors in royal tones drooped and caught fire.

Standing before a tree trunk carved to be a chair, the feet came to a sudden halt. The ground sizzled underneath the figure and the white marble began to turn grey. Making his way around the seat, the figure took in the magnificently carved animals within the trunk's sides. Every animal ever created was there, from the sea, to the sky, to the plains; every living creature had a place.

With delight and grace the Devil took the throne. In just a moment's time, something changed. As the Devil became comfortable, darkness and smoke began to pour out of the crevices of the wood like tentacles of the kraken, seeping onto the floor and spilling out across the landscape. The pillars blackened and the Devil, as he acclimated himself, became aware of something far more powerful than the throne of God.

He noticed that he was alone. No one but himself, in a place that was once beautiful before darkness over came it with fire and sorrow. He was alone and so it was. The stare of the Devil at the seat of God is a long one, one of question, one without answer.

Made in the USA
Middletown, DE
25 July 2015